Fast Eddie, King of the Bees

Robert Arellano

With Illustrations by
Marek Bennett

Akashic Books
New York

This is a work of fiction. All names, characters, places, and incidents are the product of the author's imagination. Any resemblance to real events or persons, living or dead, is entirely coincidental.

Published by Akashic Books
©2001 Robert Arellano
Illustrations ©2001 Marek Bennett
Bee illustrations by Lindsay Packer

Illustrations by Marek Bennett
Cover photo by Jeanine Tasso
Book design by richard p. morin[2] [elevated design + writing]

ISBN: 1-888451-22-X
Library of Congress Catalog Card Number: 2001087220

Akashic Books
PO Box 1456
New York, NY 10009
Akashic7@aol.com
www.akashicbooks.com

ACKNOWLEDGMENTS

The author is grateful to Marek Bennett, Matthew Derby, and Lindsay Packer for their spirited rapport in preparation of the novel manuscript.

For Mother

Don't ask me where I come from. I myself should never have asked. The question has gotten me into all sorts of trouble. I should have just kept driving that excursion bus between casinos, playing video games in Paramus, showing off for throw money on the Common, pulling purses and picking pockets across the Beast. The problem is, the question asked me. Every morning as a child I awoke with that eerie refrain. It looped in my head until the hour I distracted myself with the butterflies of a sidewalk show, the heart race of a snatch-and-chase. Each day the volume amplified until finally, even after lunch and an afternoon full of distractions, the question would not ebb, but instead, by the time my voice began cracking, found itself spoken out loud in front of Shep. Shep, a sightless hustler from Southie, was my makeshift Fagin, my only pal. He trained the youngest by pretending grift was a game, supplying his own billfold. If Shep detected promise then off you went, an independent contractor in his ranks of sticky-fingered freelancers.

As a toddler, I appeared barefoot and blinking at his rat's nest and Shep tapped me for a more conspicuous routine. "What can you do?" The rest of the road rats, witnessing my mute reaction, laughed uproariously. Shep reached out to see what was up. He could not believe his hands. I had screwed legs up behind shoulders, crossed ankles at the back of my neck, and left fabulous feet flapping above my head. "Holy cow!" said Shep, squeezing, "they're thick as tenderloins!" I can't remember where I learned that early trick, but my performance proves I already knew the props were show-worthy. My feet were, in fact, huge, but as an infant I was unashamed. They seemed separate, like shoes, although I knew they were not removable. They were two long dogs that followed me everywhere I went.

A true scavenger, Shep kept a mental index of everything he had ever picked out of the trash. He sent a veteran rat to go fetch an old pair of enormous sports shoes from his dumpster-dive archive. My eyes lit up. They were so oversized they might have belonged to a circus clown. Bright red fabric uppers extended all the way to laced high-tops. Red ankles bore emblems commemorating a long-lost century-20 legend whose legacy had likely been buried beneath a host of successors' in the annals of the Basketball Hall of Fame. Here at the apex of retro footwear, the name remained conspicuously inscribed in stitched script: CHUCK TAYLOR. It was a perfect fit. Shep showed me how to tie them and I took them for a spin, divulging my nearsightedness by bumping into the wall. Belying blindness, Shep had selected optometry for a hobby. He memorized charts and dispensed from his sidewalk stand of looted lenses by correlating patients' readings with drawers organized by prescription. Shep set me up with a pair of thick, vintage frames. The glasses, together with the sneakers, made our Cinderella story complete.

From the start, we enjoyed a filial rapport, Shep with his tactile acuity and me with my phenomenal flexibility. Flipping bottle caps back and forth at our first rehearsal, we shared a natural rhythm, syncopated and contrapuntal. Shep sightless and threadbare; I, nearsighted and, by my infancy, effectively deaf and dumb: Together we had just the right chemistry for street theater.

Earlier that day, one of the rats had pilfered a case of ginseng juice. Shep counted the empties he had amassed, decided to call me Eddie for eight, and we began feeling our way through a rudimentary routine.

"Step right up!" Shep called on the Common. "It's Baby Eddie, preschool pretzel-boy!" I puttered around on the heels of my hands, grinning goofily at anyone whose attention strayed, sneaks flopping like crimson elephant ears.

"Deux grandes baguettes!"

"Zwei grösses Bröt!"

"Will you look at those tootsies!"

"Take a minute out for mini-magic!" Shep barked. We drew droves of dupes to our spot among the mandrakes by the stump of the old hanging tree, our only props a pair of miniature steel manacles, a shrunken straitjacket, and a mysterious box beneath a sheet. "It's the babe in bondage!" Shep invited a spectator to shackle me. No sweat—or rather, lots of it. When in duress, I perspired profusely, especially at my hands and gargantuan feet. In ten seconds I was twirling those cuffs on the tip of one finger.

13

"Time for a pint-sized parlor trick," Shep bellowed. "Who'll loan Eddie a thousand-dollar bill?" People reached for G-spots. Nonchalantly, I tore the note in half—*ouch!*—and effected an instantaneous repair: *ah!* "See: same serial numbers!"

When the buzz told Shep he had assembled a good-sized gallery, he slapped them with the bondage routine. "Baby Eddie defies the confounding kiddy camisole!" Over my head went that cuffless canvas shirt, size: small/chico. I was fettered, crossed sleeves tied behind my back. Shep invited the volunteer to tighten the straps. Pointing blindly in my vicinity, Shep cried, "Eddie's been a bad boy—let's put him in the crib!" Off came the sheet at Shep's feet. What lay beneath was less like a cradle than a diver's cage, the kind that keeps out sharks. The crowd-in-the-round, built to the size that begins making cops nervous, shouted multilingual maledictions in sympathy with my organ-grinder melodrama.

"Crazy crib!"

"¡Es algo cruel!"

"Tãs ir divas smirdĩgas desas!"

A rat had found the old lobster trap washed up beneath the dilapidated docks of Inner Harbor. I climbed in. Shep padlocked the top and draped the sheet back over the crate. Buckles clinking, bars rattling, the struggle began. "No way the wound-up wonder child can get out of this one!" A couple of rat assistants hauled the whole contraption over to the edge of the Frog Pond and heaved me in. Portentous bubbles rumbled up from turgid turquoise depths. The Frog Pond is just a few feet deep, but as Shep would say forebodingly, "It only takes a teaspoon."

I would like to be able to say that my public went wild, but that was not the timbre of the times. I did not stupefy, but instead mesmerized the audience by my simple contortions, handcuff manipulation, and box tricks. It was stuff that had been around for centuries. In oglers' glazed expressions I detected the dim glimmer of recognition: The tip knew he had seen this sideshow before, or at least that it was common currency in the collective unconscious; but so too was it in his genetic programming to stop and gawk, jaw dropped, while I went through a routine, however amateurish, that I performed with devotion. Pedestrians sensed this and stayed. Most of these working stiffs were just trudging between two drudgeries: family and job, job and second job, ad nauseam. That they paused to soak up a show from a freak like me demonstrated they needed a little felicitous fallacy, anything to distract them from the daily drear that remained constant in the noisy bowels of the Beast (which was, incidentally, the only way Shep referred to the cruel metropolis), each rev and beep another sour note of the feast in which we were all mere morsels. The audience wanted illusion, and they aided me toward the end of effecting their deception. Executed with affection, a delicate diversion was welcome escape from the hard honesties of the day-to-day.

Perspiration, the universal lubricant, had allowed me to slip those shackles—which I had made sure were cinched far up on the thick parts of forearms—over wrists without a scrape. Cleaving the G had required only a concealed decoy and a canny mouth sound. Most of the straitjacket escape had been accomplished before the trap got tossed in the drink. I inflated my chest (even a kid can get a good pint of air in there) and tensed my arms the instant before the pigeon pulled the straps.

When the getaway was underway, I relaxed, exhaled, and stole a good two inches of maneuvering room. Grasping is the child's legendary first reflex, but while my more fortunate contemporaries kept busy grabbing plastic baubles whenever daddy got rattled, I applied a child's prodigious grip to metal buckles and leather cuffs. Thus, concentrating pincer power through thick sailcloth, I freed one arm and then the other. As for the cage, some things are secrets of the trade. I, quicker than the quotidian eye, dragged myself dripping from the Frog Pond, peeled off the soggy sheet, and tossed away the rattling restraints, bowing to hollers and applause.

Shep narrated my entire routine, hawk, gawk, and pass-the-hat. It was never too hard to find suckers ready to throw a few coins for this kind of thing. Old-timers like Shep remembered the boom days when there were bills for everything down to the dollar and a C was considered a lot of dough, but before I was born there had been the Age of Deregulation, the Double-O Devaluation, the Great Privatization, and all the other market affectations that left the wealthy one percent miserly and the rest of us pretty much impoverished. Now it was a self-serve world and anything less than a hundred was small change. A twenty meant a pleased patron. Tens were most common, token appreciation for a few minutes of street theater. Fives were almost an insult. A dull, dun-colored Sacagawea slug was something a self-respecting street performer might leave behind.

Shep kept everyone idling until it was time for me to scramble for the jingling metal confetti, detaining them with his trademark slogan, which lulled even the sharpest cynics with its matter-of-fact ingenuousness: "What have you got to lose?" The point was: plenty. While Shep and I supplied distraction, the other rats marked the pigeons in the pack. Every moment of the show was carefully orchestrated to provide the claque with statistics on the quarry. When Shep asked for a thousand, the rats watched not only the one who supplied the Clinton, but all those who felt for their purses or wallets. This told us who was holding enough to consider contributing a bill. With the pedestrians-turned-patrons pressing close in a circle, I amazed and astounded while my orphan siblings conspired to lighten the burden of select pockets. When the show was over and the crowd dispersed, our agents tailed their marks out from the axis along their trajectories across the hub.

Lucky for us rats was the widespread alienation among the plebitude stocking our pantries. It would have blown the lid off our operation entire if on any given weekday a handful of the picked pockets and grabbed bags of the Beast had gotten together and, after some small talk, discovered what they all had in common: Baby Eddie's spectacle shortly before the take.

Since the beginning, I had understood the practices surrounding my pediatric profession to be a little unorthodox, but I managed to convince myself that, however bastardized by my orphan brothers to promote the conditions of easy crime, my prestidigitation preserved its integrity. Besides, growing into it as I had from an impressionable age, the career appeared to me not just as the only possible job, but as a sort of calling.

The Beast was one big Chinatown that had sprawled into South Station, the financial district, and what had formerly been known as the North End. Sooty, sparking skyscrapers loomed above our barrel-bottom dominion in ominous, opulent decadence, but you can bet a road rat never stopped to notice their gothic majesty. It was not in our wiring to admire, much less look up. So little sunlight filtered down to the street that reds and yellows got subtracted from the spectrum. If a helicopter ran out of juice, missing all the pads on the way down, and let a rich man descend upon the Beast, the city might seem to him like some awesome Atlantis, the indigo hues that come along with plumbing the deepest troughs like sinking into an altogether-other medium.

We rats were kept busy running errands, picking pockets, and bringing Shep meals in exchange for nothing but room and board, an occasional keep-the-change, and frequent epistemological floggings, which were as close as we got to affection. Nevertheless, Shep provided for his orphan cadets in a cozy, condemned candy factory near Kendall Square in Cambridge. After an old sign on the roof that had lost a letter or two, rats called his flophouse the Nec—rhymes with "mess". Gone were the days when homelessness had been more or less an exception and the most destitute had had access to shelters, group homes, orphanages, and adoption programs. Health care had become something for the ultra-rich. For rats, medical attention meant fly-by-night storefronts operated by drunken quacks with expired licenses who were nevertheless enough in demand to require all-day waits. Prevention meant not letting oneself get run over or shot. Shep was pretty fair compared to the dozen or so alternatives available to boys in the Beast. (Although occasionally a pack master might arrange a back-alley mixer with a matron and her mice, there were no coed crews. Guardians for both genders agreed packs produced more income without the drama of that most distracting difference.) By enlisting with Shep, we knew we could depend on him to supply the basic necessities: a leaky roof, our daily grub, and a bed of old *Globes*. Pack masters were beholden to a big cheese in Jersey who managed operations throughout the entire Northeast. He called himself Apple Jack, and he made sure everyone on the street understood that words wouldn't rhyme and the sun wouldn't rise without AJ's say-so.

On weekends at the Nec there was school. In the Beast, Saturdays and Sundays were zero-volume days for road rats: worse, they could be liabilities. Not only did S-day operations fail to produce rat revenue, they increased the risk of even the best getting caged. There was a fraction of the scratch on the streets, but just as many badges soaking up overtime. Most masters gave packs the weekend off, which was how fidgety kids got into trouble with drugs, violent rivalries, or extraneous operations, but on those two consecutive days with the pair of cherished names, while children of fortune spent outrageous allowances on expensive toys, Shep's rats recited Shakespeare and plotted algebraic operations. Other packs poked fun at our school days, but among those rats literacy was limited to a few street names and mathematics was capped at the fingers: ten for the boss, one for me.

After breakfast on Saturdays and Sundays, Shep would rattle his favorite prop, a tin cup blooming with a fresh bouquet of colored pencils, and call roll. Anyone absent was locked out that night. Attendance was invariably one hundred percent, although I remember one time a new kid tried getting away with having his name called by a stoolie. The other pupils had not so much as snickered; still, the stooge went down with the truant. "Does Scotch Ronny sound that much like Papo the Bullet to you," Shep had said to the class, "or just because I'm blind you think I'm deaf and stupid, too?" Ten seconds of terrifying silence. The brash newcomer, who would later become a magnificent critic of French existentialism, stepped out from the stairwell. He had perhaps been prepared for exposure, but certainly could not have foreseen the consequences. What would it be? Detention? Expulsion? No: Leaning on the easel, Shep told Papo to take his seat. The boss let a single tear drop damply from beneath his ebony shades. All the rats brooded silently through Shep's unusually subdued lecture. It took the entire morning for a great, avocado-sized pit of sadness to dissolve in my throat.

Shep started us on basic lessons of grammar and math, but as he saw it, long-term understanding of how white-collar investments would factor into our gray-collarless levies required trigonometry and calculus, and getting a leg up on rival packs' business plans involved not just the ability to read, but also powers of composition, rhetoric, and oratory. He turned the concentrated education of his charges into a personal obsession.

Shep bestowed enhanced responsibility on restless students. The new boy who couldn't sit still during drama class, for instance, would be selected to play Viola in *Twelfth Night*. We went twelve hours each day with an hour break mid-afternoon sometimes forfeited for a working lunch of barreling through a tricky proof or rehearsing a particularly piquant scene. There was plenty of play early in the school day to bring energies to equilibrium. "Sink time!" Shep would shout, and let us let off steam. After a little rabble rousing—some rooftop tag or a side-alley game of capture the flag—we would get back to our army-surplus e-books. As the pack fluctuated between twenty and thirty rats, the student-teacher ratio remained comparable to that of blue-blood private schools. Reasonable class sizes facilitated across-the-board participation. On, weeknights, advanced students were required to help prepare lessons. We signed up for Net time on an old term Shep had dug out of the basement—"No games or porn!" Before lights out, there were compulsory study hours that Shep monitored like a bat.

I sat at the front of the class in that ancient candy factory and soaked up Shep's lectures while frequently squeegeeing confectionery dust from my glasses. My favorite subject was civics. Back in the early 2000s, city, state, and federal courts had gotten clogged with decades of backed-up litigation. Now it was up for grabs whether anyone submitting a new case— even a healthy, non-smoking female in her teens—would see the docket in her lifetime. Cynicism reigned and justice had become something Americans learned to live without. Taxes that were supposed to be earmarked for social services never found their way to the street.

Transportation departments and divisions of motor vehicles had been dissolved and roads crumbled in gross disrepair everywhere but the upscale suburbs. Since the highways had been privatized, mechanics retooled chassis and suspensions to withstand the most punishing conditions. The whole region had come to function like a pock-marked Autobahn. Entrepreneurial garages beefed up tow patrols. Politicians proudly invoked a great tradition of New England's categorical cartographic indifference by reminding their constituencies that driving is a privilege and if you didn't already know how to get someplace—from beguiling Berkshires traffic circles to the snarl around Harvard Square—you probably didn't belong.

It might take a PhD from MIT to follow Mass Ave and Mount Auburn across Cambridge, but of the motorist minority that remained, people who could afford gas at a hundred dollars a gallon, few complained. A capacity to cope automotively was twisted into the Brahmins' inbred DNA. Ever since the days when an elevated highway had bisected the heart of downtown, drivers had become accustomed to cutthroat merges at inner city onramps, anti-gravity escape velocities at exits, and four-hour commutes from within a ten-mile radius. Another thing about auto apartheid: It kept us undesirables in our place. If you flew into the Beast, it was only to wet your beak. The rich preyed on the poor with the same controls as ever—ghetto rentals, extortionate retail, usurious utilities—but now they had honed the getaway. Long distances over ramshackle roadways kept the one-percenters safe in their suburban communities. Pavement conditions, at first harrowing, smoothed the further you got from the city. You took the high road out of the Beast because you had somewhere better to be. For us, the people of the streets, roads were nothing but rubble.

Back in late century 20, the old chief plunderers had given shape to the most ambitious and expensive public works project in the 222 years since their domestic-levy alternative to Mother England's taxation without representation. They could have at least had a little fun with it—the Pike Gets a Dike, Scrubba-Dub-Hub, the Boss Colostomy—but the hucksters who ran this part of the world at the time, juvenile goofballs of European ancestry, were satisfied with the most insipid of images rendered in primitive and faintly phallocentric nursery rhyme: the Big Dig. It was pretty typical that, sixteen billion dollars later at its not-so-grand opening in 2004, the Central Artery/Tunnel trafficked nothing but trouble: loose joints, egregious leaks, all-out cave-ins. Those imaginative Massholes again adapted, turning service roads and bypasses into main express routes. Between South and North Ends, for instance, they took the Ted Williams (the first tunnel constructed in the Dig debacle and one of the few pieces of the outlandish plan that remained intact) into East Beast and the Callahan back. To get over the Charles on the cable-stayed bridge, they tore across town on Mass Ave, that no-man's alley where the down-and-out patronized dangerous diversions like Commonwealth Drag Track, Christian Science Jet Ski, and Symphony Hall Paintball. The underground expressway had been exposed for its real public work: a grotto of graft. In the end, the taxpayer had gotten the shaft, and the substructure was ultimately condemned.

Now, shoe-shiners and sewer workers spoke of the displaced people who had gone down into the abandoned tunnels and carved out a new counterculture, calling the labyrinth in the Beast's knothole home. Their chief contractor was a mysterious misfit known only as Levis. A Harvard dropout who combined the art of Joseph Beuys, the anthroposophy of Rudolf Steiner, and the Zapatista doctrine of Subcomandante Marcos, Levis had modeled the hive on his B-minus project from a seminar in emergency architecture. He blocked off all the shafts constructed in the 1990s and turned the network into an alternative empire. Along with his wife Jocy and her brother Cray, Levis had formed a subterranean colony fomenting secession. Hundreds of bottom-feeders, indignant over being deprived a fair shake of change on the surface, had gone down under to join the orphaned race. Through sewer grates and exhaust vents, the low thrum of revolution could be heard coming up from beneath the streets. The expatriates called the rogue nation Dig City.

Unlike aboveground efforts at independence, Dig City was built in the establishment's underbelly, so there were no holistic alternatives to those of the adversary. Solar: nope. Hydro: hardly a trickle. Wind: Let me show you the door. Dig City depended on stolen stores of alternating and direct current from above. Discreet chains of pipe and cable appended to the bases and foundations of the Beast's skyscrapers provided a vast network of pirated utilities, from electricity and network services to natural gas and plumbing. The mission was similar to that of road rat diplomacy: to appropriate resources when and where they're needed. It was an entire misfit metropolis on the grift. The culture to which they were counter was made up of the same guys I agitated as a rat, except this time the resistance was directed at the level of their offices and conference rooms instead of simple, street-level pocket fare. What was this siphoning of energy off the back—or, better, bottom—of the staid old Beast if not one massive billfold lift?

Shep concluded his lesson on the sprawling squat built in the sham artery: "You don't want to go there." Even if we had, it wouldn't have been easy. Networked portals sealed the seven tunnel entrances Mass Highway had left behind. To program security, Levis had recruited the infamous hacker Miss Spinks, a legendary boxer's cross-dressing great-grandson who had made a notorious name for herself by generating the puckish

GENDERBENDER virus. From south of the city among the abandoned train tracks and the overgrowth-choked flower exchange to more than a mile away near the sullen, slouching cement works, nobody could get in or out of Dig City without Spinks's authorization.

Most rats weren't interested in what lay beneath. After all, there was enough for them to focus on along the X and Y axes. I sometimes sat on the Summer Street railing and daydreamed about the Z. In the smoke-scented dusk of the Beast in spring-time, I dangled my two sandbags above the shut-up tunnel mouth and wondered what kids with mothers and fathers made of such wistful perfumes. Some infants stand free on two feet at six months while others dawdle on into their second orbits. Whatever time it takes, not long after upending us with that grand cosmic shift, nature permeates child consciousness with a devious inclination. What just-ambulatory tyke has not recklessly tested the newly-acquired talent, running with ecstatic abandon from parents who first coo, then shout, and finally squawk in the blood-curdling caw of the kraken? I have seen toddlers no older than two outrun mamas and papas on the street. If it's known as the terrible age, then it has to do with the grown-ups' terror-stricken response to the fulsomest infant revolt, the first, the ultimate rebellion—final, for when the individual elects to flee protector, then no longer can he or she properly be spoken of as in infancy. Somewhere in the world on a busy sidewalk, right now, such an incubus is on the run from mom and dad. The race has begun!

As I cannot recall crawling, I am pretty certain that a precocious podiatric endowment had rendered me erectus earlier than most, ambulatory soon after, and that I had, perhaps well before a single lap around the sun, adapted this science to the art of sprinting. Whatever the mystery about how I had ended up on the street, there was one thing I knew for certain: A road rat to the core, I had been born scurrying. Although never certain of my exact age, at various junctions throughout my career I had marveled at how I had begun so young and made it so far without ever going anywhere. When, like my fellow rats who were sure they were six, new incisors had pushed out my old front teeth, I had enough sense to say, "How did I ever live this way when I was three?" When hair began growing in all the places that it betides a twelve-year-old, it became: "What was that little boy of six doing daily on these streets?" A lot of my acquiescence could be attributed to Shep, with his sadistic charisma, reigning over the rats in the Nec from one day to the next. He was as feckless as he was offensive and, however obnoxious his behavior, his irrepressible ambition remained infectious. But I knew all the inertia had something to do with me, too, and with my predilection for kinesis.

That fugitive kid who has just discovered flight, the one we left running down the street a minute ago, perhaps ends up giving in. He is caught, coddled, scolded, what have you, and he lets the devious knowledge of his capacity to escape submerge, sublimate itself, and stew into all sorts of murderous, incestual, or otherwise pathological longings until the day he ditches the nest or else drastically acts. Or, outpacing authority, the child escapes and emerges into a city full of strange faces, a world glaring in his eyes with the peril and possibility of the sun reflecting off a car hood on a hot summer day. Not so different from the apron-laced naïf, that child just keeps running. That child is me.

On light-traffic days, when Shep managed operations from his sidewalk optician booth in Back Bay, I would bring him a grinder from the sandwich cart down the street. He scarfed his sandwiches lustily, swallowing shreds of wax paper along with the comestible contents, mayo dripping down his stubbly chin and embellishing the mural of past meals across the front of his coat. He didn't care. "It's a symbol of my extraordinary gusto for the regional cuisine," he said. Shep always articulated big words syllabically for the benefit of the pack. "Ex-tra-or-din—," he would say, "airy like the wind. Words are soul food for the chicken, which is why I'm always talking and often spitting." Shep wanted us to use extraordinary words proudly just like he did, although he also had a knack for arresting vernacular, as on the hand-scrawled sign tacked to his stand: "If you're mean enough to steal from the blind . . . FUCK YOU!"

One lunch break, in the moment of tranquillity that succeeded his ravenous repast, I asked Shep the big question. "Where did I come from?"

"Aw, Eddie," he said, "what's the use in wondering?"

Road rats were a race that went mostly by aliases, and there were so many of us in the Beast that it was futile to try finding out origins. Most knew nothing about the conditions of their orphaning. Few of them cared. It was their daily takes, their stomachs, and their standings with Shep that concerned them. Certainly, there was plenty for us to preoccupy ourselves with between raising the rent and staying out of jail. Still, I had to know. Who were my mother and father? How had they died, if they were dead? Why had they left me in this hard world with so little to recommend me?

Shep laid into me with one of his trademark rants. "It's like trying to figure out where a coin came from. Someone baits you with it, handing it to you and craftily asking what you think. You say, 'Render unto Caesar what is Caesar's,' and absent-mindedly pocket the piece . . . "

Speaking of which, there was a coin. It was my lucky charm, good or bad. I had carried it on me ever since I could remember. I found it at the bottom of my trouser pocket one day like it had always been there. Maybe it was thrown to me as chump change after an escape, or given up by a passing aristocrat when I hadn't even been panhandling, or it was useless, alien change some cashier had unloaded from the till. Perhaps it had been sewn discretely into my dirty denim by fastidious old Shep so as to erupt from the fabric on precisely the day I needed to discover it.

". . . Or you shake it out of the piggy bank and try to make it to the fair to get some trivial figurine for a girl who doesn't know you exist—only they're shutting all the booths down, the vendors are condescending, and the tchotchke feels like death in your cold hand . . . "

It was American, from before the time ten- and twenty-dollar slugs became common currency. It was not the sort of thing I could get anything for, unless on some off-chance I bumped into an eccentric collector, but someone that loaded never made it down to the street to meet a rat like me. He was locked all day in a cubicle high up in a skyscraper talking about money he never saw and brought to a ghastly mansion at night with a warm, perfumed wife and a brood of little monsters who complained about the insufficient crispness of the breakfast cereals in the refectories of the gated schools where they were prepped to take daddy's place. Worthless, you bet, but all the same I developed a bit of affection for the piece. It had been struck out of a copper which, when rubbed between fingers, could be made to glimmer. The brassy cast made me picture chimneys choking sky with smoke and, behind the hazy horizon, a defeated sun glowing a moment before going out. That was the color of my coin, and I liked it. Every day the finish tarnished anew, and every night I buffed it to a warm, worn shine.

". . . Or you fish through a curbside sewer grate for the ticket to enter a wacked-out chocolatier's nightmare factory: What do you know! an enchanted token . . ."

How was I supposed to figure out where I had gotten it? On the head was a profile of the guy who had been on the old paper fives when bills were still printed in such low denominations. Lincoln, I think. Around the outside: "IN GOD WE TRUST/LIBERTY/2001." Tails, there was a reproduction of a columnar structure. It was maybe what the famed, pillared Parthenon once looked like, with a couple of erect figures on the steps and one smack in the center. "UNITED STATES OF AMERICA/E PLURIBUS UNUM/ONE CENT," plus a minuscule "FG" at the lower right. That was it. The edge was not reeded, but slightly raised to a lip. In an attempt to curb Shep's contumely, I pressed One Cent into his palm. "Can you guess how many people there are on it?"

Shep rubbed the face under his thumb. "One dumb honky with a stupid-looking beard."

"A profile on the head, yes. But check tails."

Shep grimaced, rubbed some more. "Oh yeah. All right. There's someone teeny sitting between the pillars. Is this worth anything?"

"No, not that I know."

"Then why are you wasting my time?"

"Can't you feel it? On the steps? There are two more people standing there."

He squeezed a little harder. "Naw, Eddie. Those are posts."

"If they were posts they would be centered, right? While the left one's just slightly more inward of the third column."

"You're fooling yourself, kid. They're posts. And those trails leading up the steps are chains."

"Let me see that."

I squinted through thick lenses. Sure enough, a faint, raised wisp emerged from each of the figures and arced up the steps.

"They're not chains!" I said. "They're . . . I don't know what they are, but there are three people on the back."

Deep in the black lagoons of his perennial dark lenses, I could almost see Shep's eyes ignite with recognition. "Oh, I get it, Eddie." He beamed a brilliant white smile. "Mommy, daddy, and baby in the cradle."

"Shut up, Shep."

That evening, with all the rats gathered for supper, Shep announced, referring to the freshest recruit, "Billy needs a name." Every rat got a pack alias. It usually consisted of the forename complemented by some kind of qualifier: superlative, alliterative, rhymed, or otherwise ornamental. "And," Shep said, proposing like a sadistic Magwich what I most feared, "we have to pick a new one for Eddie. 'Baby' doesn't cut it anymore."

Billy predictably proposed for himself "the Kid." He thought it was original, and to Shep it had that ring of something you maybe heard before.

In my case, the moniker might not have been intended as a means of persecution. As we all know, there is no insult unless one is taken. Even the cruelest words miss the mark if the target is unmoved. I could have stood almost any slam: Sweaty Eddie, Pretzel Puss, obvious taunts of the four-eyes' variety, but in my head I had already picked the nightmare name, the tag I was sure I would not be able to live down should my colleagues ever decide to dub me as such. All it took was the kid—I should say Kid—Billy, brimming with pride at his recent induction, burnished by the flush of inclusion, blurting the obvious, inevitable sobriquet. Thus was born a nickname that would, like wet shit in the treads of my too-tight Chuck Taylors, stick. The other rats might have meant it at first affectionately and tossed the name around only briefly. In their mouths, it might have supplied a temporary anaesthetic to eradicate embarrassment and ever after deny the deformity. If I had only had the presence to propose an alternative I might have avoided humiliation, but instead I pursed my lips and began to perspire. Self-consciousness was the midwife of my disgrace. When my cheeks flushed red and glasses got all steamed, Billy the Kid smelled blood and turned it into an opportunity for mirth too good to miss. He repeated the dreadful designation. The rest of the pack's hysterical laughter was adequate to register as unanimous ratification. I knew from the pitch of their reaction that, with relentless hilarity and for many months to come, I would be hailed—"Hey!"—this way—"Eddie Feet!"

There was plenty that preoccupied me as a foundling, but

nothing so much as self-consciousness over my terrific trotters, and, in paired inversion, one other thing: the little matter of where they had come from. Over years of amazing exhibitions, all of my obsessive exertion—sitting Indian style, standing pigeon-toed, sporting bell-bottoms that, when I stomped fleetly down the street, tolled far over the toes—had been unable to obscure the exoticism of the extremities. It would not have been so bad if I had merely hated these ungainly ungulae, but as it stood I was a little protective of them, for they must have been bestowed by someone, and that person was half my obsession. Maybe they belonged to a clumsy father who helplessly tripped over them every time he tried to dance, or perhaps to an athletic grandma who as a girl had flopped to an obscure, turn-of-the-century gold in Sydney. They were my only inheritance, and I held onto the hope that someday, somebody—a prince bearing a castaway crystal slipper that could double as a punchbowl—might come along and lay claim to them and me.

By the dimming light of the drafty Nec, a suffocating survival instinct surfaced amid the general wretchedness for one last gasp of gumption: What would be required to reverse the damage of the naming? The irrefutable response: Provide a substitution for the sources of my scandal. The rest of the rats rocked in their chairs and ducked looks under the table, goggling at the objects of ridicule, while I covered my crimson face with my hands. Thus, in the instant following my moment of greatest desolation, there arrived a dram of alacrity which buffeted the traumatic blow. Fingers vertical-blind shading the shame, a glimmer of hope somehow as-yet-unextinguished allowed me to perceive that deliverance resided in those selfsame digits, and I resolved to apply myself to the surest method of displaying manual dexterity. It was not want of money, then, that led me to a more immediate involvement with crime, but the conviction that overcoming Billy's pedestrian insult would require displacing cheap slander with genuine legend.

Over the detestable remains of that ruined, ruinous dinner, I whispered, "Shep, I want to pick."

"I don't think that's such a good idea, Eddie," Shep said, "what with all you bring in just doing your escape act, not to mention what the other rats take after the marks go their separate ways."

"Come on, boss, I'm getting too big for the crib. Think about what I could do with sleight of hand applied to pockets." Shep paused and for a moment considered me, the idea, and the overall aura. With his all-seeing fingers he reached up and rubbed his temples. I had raised the specter of a great take. Now, to finish the job, I spooked him with regurgitation of his own pet disclaimer: "What have you got to lose?"

I lined up with the rest of the pack for the nightly trim. Long hair can conceal the magician's concern, half-occlude a beguiling expression, or provide figurative mist for a smoke-and-mirrors moment, but the pickpocket must keep close-cropped to guard against a grab. Shep's post-supper grooming clinic was harrowing for the prospect of losing a lobe, but compulsory if you planned to pick the next day. Although we rats trembled, Shep never so much as nicked. Scissoring sibilant air, he said of his talent, "Shear feeling."

Next, I gave myself a manicure. For good reason has the magician's trademark toilet long mandated a set of elegant, toothy nails: They provide ten teeny, discrete cubbies for secluding minuscule tools at one's literal fingertips. An average prestidigitator's arsenal might include monkey grease, conjurer's wax, coiled hairpins, skeleton keys, balled elastics, dash of saltpeter, topical anaesthetic, chloroform resin, collapsible hypodermic, sneezing powder, sandpaper, smoke dust, morphine, mandrake, and half a dozen other accessories and essences to produce an entire battery of theatrical effects. Pronounced talons are essential to the art of legerdemain, supplying endless potential for deception of a gullible volunteer and credulous audience. Properly polished, nails provide arms-length reflectors for discerning the suit of a pigeon's playing card or giving off the eerie impression of having eyes in the back of one's head. Sufficiently sharpened, gelatin ends can cut through the toughest twine. For illusionists as well as certain larcenists (in a pinch, a seasoned second-story man might employ points like lock picks), long claws are de rigueur.

On the other hand, you have the picker of pockets. A tip that is hooked, split, or even just microscopically sharded can perilously hang him up. He can be the slickest slipper in the universe, with the fuzz shaved off the back of his knuckles and joints buffed to a bowling-ball shine, but one stray thread getting caught on an imperfect nail will send pickpocket howling *ouch!* and his mark hollering for help. Who has not heard of the attempt in which a messy-mitted misfit gets snagged on a fretfully frayed hem, tying up himself and his victim in a degrading tango on a busy corner until the law finally arrives to rescue them, applying cuffs before clippers to the self-captured man's hands? With this legendary loser in mind, I pruned my performer's pincers.

On the eve of my audition, dourly sporting a buzz and brandishing a fair pair of filed fingers, I, newly and ruefully dubbed Eddie Feet, went out to get myself some running shoes. I already knew the ones I wanted. The pair I had set my sights on were not in a store window, and they certainly were not for sale. They had gone up a few weeks earlier in the Beacon Hill slums. There had been an old pair there as long as I could remember, but these huge shoes, in keen lime green, were brand new. Visibly, the sneaks were no smaller than my size— they certainly don't come any bigger—and best of all they were free for the taking . . . if you didn't mind climbing a utility pole.

I sat watching the tenement from a stoop across Beacon Street. All the rats had heard of Mano, a seasoned hacker who controlled most of the Beast's cybertropic trade. He programmed and peddled some of the more sought-after prescriptions, a digital pharmacopoeia administered transdermally for an electro-synaptic high. This stuff was so hot it had to be kept off the Net. Users picked up a RAM chip from the dealer in person, concealed it in a nether crevice of clothing, and scurried away to jack in on a private term. Fixes you could shut off or on with a keystroke, cybertropics weren't physically addictive, but the powers that be, pissed they couldn't get their hands on a cut of the profits, outlawed them as subversive, potentially revolutionary.

Mano's customers came and went through the unnumbered entrance of the inconspicuous walk-up. The sign dangling high above the curb said all they needed to know—if they were in the know. Fat laces slung over electrical wires, the shoes were a flag for cybertropic services supplied covertly inside a dilapidated brownstone. It was uncertain what else Mano took care of in his HQ. The breadth of his clandestine projects was beyond the scope of rats going about our day-to-day business. Worse than a mere outlaw, Mano was a wild card, someone who, for all his involvement in activities both licit and il-, you could be sure was not on anybody's side but his own. Besides, Shep prohibited cybertropics, and getting caught consorting with Mano meant immediate ejection from the Nec.

A low-rider rolled up, dropped hydraulics, and parked. The driver got out and entered the apartment. Having determined after careful observation that each deal lasted a minimum of eight minutes, I took my chance in the lull. Scaling the base of the pole, I climbed cautiously over metal cleats, keeping clear of wood well-splintered by repairmen's boots. My supple old Chuck Taylors hung tough, giving their all in their last starring role. For maximum extension I had to go all the way to the top and poke my head between the lines in the direction of the shoes' lofty perch. "AIR," read the polymer uppers, emblazoned with vinyl swooshes like the wings of a god. The namesake of the style, Michael, must have been the equivalent of Mercury in his day, for these high-tops could not have been designed for a mere mortal. They were gum-soled gun ships, canvas Cadillacs.

Aloft, sighting down the wires, I felt a little breeze at my back that I momentarily, queasily took for a good sign. I leaned my Adam's apple against the leeward line and reached rigidly with my right hand. Fully stretched, I still could not grasp the coveted sneaks. Maybe a millimeter remained to obtain the tantalizing prize, lightly rocking in the wind. I did not try my left arm, which after years of street theater I already knew to be a smidgen shorter. Had I been carrying some implement—a pen, a key, or even a paper clip—I would have been able to make contact. But I had nothing. How had I let myself come so grossly unprepared? There wasn't anything down on the deserted street that could aid me and besides, according to my biological hourglass, at least three hundred seconds had gone by during the current transaction. Even if I scrambled down and broke off a car antenna, I wouldn't make it back up in time, and with lockout at the Nec less than thirty minutes away it would be impossible for me to return before my momentous morning foray. Wryly, I considered that the inch I had clipped from my nails no more than an hour earlier would have generously compensated for the infinitesimal distance separating me from success. In an avalanche of bleak, unspecific musings, my entire short life seemed to be an adumbration of such inauspicious inversions and confounded effects.

Stuck atop a stick above Beacon Street, I hit upon an alternative. Since the day I had first detected the suspended treasure, the lower shoe had plunged precipitously, practically upsetting the pendular equilibrium of the pair. I could reach up and shake the wire in question, possibly jostling the sneakers free. I knew, by a convoluted strain of superstition that had come to dominate my impulse in the clutch over the years, that it was do or die, and so I resolved to give it a try. First, against all hope, in an absent old compulsive gesture, I double-checked my pockets. Well, whataya know?—lucky One Cent. At least, at one time I had dubbed it lucky. Now I had the option of putting the trinket to the test with a superstitious little flip, giving the chip of worthless ore the opportunity to serve as my deliverance. I had perhaps seconds left. "What'll it be, Abe? Make a monkey of myself with the coconut-tree routine or take a desperation shot at the buzzer?" "I'd say go with plan B, E," came a sober voice, internally—so I muttered ignorantly an idiot incantation, *E Pluribus Unum*, which on my lips in that essential instant felt altogether holy, and gave the coin a toss to

find out whether One Cent held any fortune after all—
"considering you've already almost toasted yourself." "What's
that supposed to mean?" Like a lightening bolt it hit me.
A wary, whiplash-victim's glance at the junction box over
my shoulder confirmed my suspicion: Holy shit! I just about
created a circuit! The sparking imprecations of Shep's
attention-jerking science lectures came back to me with a jolt.
Upon ascending to the topmost rung, I had narrowly inserted
my head and left my neck bristling between two lines which, if
touched together, would, in an instant, have my goose cooked.
Without thinking to lift my chin from the first, I had just about
reached up to grasp the extension of wire-the-second.

One Cent sunk—*swish!*—right into the nigh insole. With
its gram of ballast, it sent the low shoe swinging. The sneaker
swayed for a moment, then all of a sudden slid the scales of
justice just a whisper in my favor. Laces slithered, shoes spun,
and the whole shebang twirled off the wires and toppled end
over end through the air to street—*clop! clop!*

I could not move. For close to ten minutes I had been, as I
remained at that very mortal moment, an excellent candidate
for conduit of awesome amperes. Now how the hell would I get
out, considering the copious—and especially conductive—
saline pouring down my brow? Already having served an oblivious sentence in this high-voltage stockade, I dared not peek
down at the death-dealing cables. Just the crackling of the air
told me one wire practically tickled my chin while the other
almost touched my scruff. If I touched both at once, I would
end up one roasted bird. I could almost hear Shep committing
my ashes to the bay: "Hadn't that shmuck learned anything in
Introductory Street Physics?"

The instant before my glasses fogged up, I, practically paralyzed, caught a glimpse of them coming out of the undercover drugstore: first the driver, then, behind him, hulking in the doorway like a demented reject from the Patriots' defensive line, Mano, nonchalantly palming a basketball. His hands were huge. He probably could have crushed someone's skull single-handedly, literally. I heard Mano dribble the ball on the way to the car. The two got in, slammed doors. Engine roared, hydraulics hissed, and subwoofers kicked in, supplying a throbbing drum for the hunt. When they started to drive away, I thought I might have escaped the predators' detection, if not the lattice of electrocution. Squealing brakes—headlights had caught the upset shoes, planted in a pothole. There was a sickening measure of eight booming bass beats as from the front seat eyes plotted the function from street to sky: high-tops . . . utility pole . . . power line . . . dodo in his nest. The beat got loud when the window rolled down. The mad scientist who synthesized the most sought-after cybertropics in all the Northeast couldn't be bothered to get out of the car, much less climb the pole to collar a petty thief, but he did crane his head out to shout, "What the fuck are you doing?"

In vertical traction, all I could do was stall, and my only medium was my mouth. "Shopping for sneaks," I said.

"Those Jordans might just fit." Mano held the palmed ball out the window. "My homey and I were going to play some one-on-one, but why don't we make it a game of ghost? Catch!" He hurled.

It was a good thing I couldn't see through misted glasses: I might have flinched. The ball ricocheted off the coupling under my nose, causing the brittle solder to snap. In reckless reflex, I reached, caught the rubber casing of the power line, and, Tarzan-style, took a swing on a thousand-watt vine. I understood why the king of the jungle made that exotic call: He wasn't showing off, he was shitting his pants. Trailing the charged fray like an electric eel, I sailed by the car window and set fire to the tuft of hair beside Mano's right ear. He ducked inside and boxed the flames while I spun 180 and landed on my feet on the low-rider hood, leaving two dinosaur prints in the steel. Looking through the windshield at each other, we shared a collective shudder: Mano in the passenger seat with one singed sideburn, his hoops partner holding the wheel, and I on top of the engine. Still holding the insulated cable, I sprung down to pavement and jammed the end of the wire into the hood ornament. Mano reached for the door handle and it sparked in his hand. "Motherfucker!"

I have always hated it when people say that. As obscenity, it seems senseless, and yet the intent is always so brutal. The car abruptly jerked backwards, crumpling the back bumper against the base of the pole, but the juice stayed stuck in the jack. Mano dove across the driver's lap and punched the emergency brake. "Dumbass! you're going to get us short-circuited!" He growled out the window, "Come on, kid, unplug that shit!"

I wiped the condensation from my lenses. I was so overcome from being alive and in possession that, shuddering on rubber legs before the hard-won award, I flouted the urgency to leave the scene, kicked off the old Chuck Taylors, and tried on my prize right there. Nerves fritzed, my body spasmed as if I had just gone through shock treatment. Nevertheless, a magician's nimble fingers took only a second to unknot the bind tying high-tops together. The shoes had barely been out of the box, but after getting left out in the rain a few times were not so stiff, as if by nature broken in, and they fit my feet like second skin. Pressing into the insole, I could feel at my right heel where that auspicious little coin had come to rest. Not only had One Cent sunk the sought-after shoes, but, at the essential juncture, its charmed discovery had saved my tail. Had it not been for little Lincoln, I would certainly have acted, in my defeatist distraction, on the unfortunate impulse to grab the reaper's bait. That talisman was much luckier than I had surmised.

I cast a cursory glance at my old Chuck Taylors bereft in the gutter, offering a curt and final salute. Galvanized inside the car, Mano tried to cajole me into revoking the voltage. "Come on, bro," the big bruiser cooed. "I won't hurt you. Help us out and I'll tell you a secret." I pushed the glasses up the bridge of my nose, turned, and strolled off in my new shoes, bouncing Mano's ball across the Common, taking time to smell the mandrakes.

Shep and I stalked through the streets outside South Station. After a wired, sleepless night, I had risen with a sense of fatalistic dread. I did not feel hungry, but my stomach turned and churned with a raucous racket that I was sure would give me away. Shep, smiling his insufferable grin, said, "Damn! boy! Didn't you get enough for breakfast?" knowing full well I had skipped the morning meal as well as the demoralizing dinner the night before. My palms profusely perspired, which Shep somehow sensed. "Axle grease," he called it. "Good for manual transmission. Go on, sweat it up, Eddie. Enough of that lube and not even the lint will stick. Just don't drop the chop." My heart? A frenetic lab rat raced Sisyphian laps on a treadmill smack in the middle of my ribcage. The scientist-sadists had him on more speed than anybody, man or mouse, had ever been given, so the entire mechanism—hub, spokes, and squeaky, lopsided wheel—was shimmying on skids through the cavity in my chest, lurching ever so slightly, unbearably left. Long had I lingered as the pretty boy of the pack, performing decoy deceits while the real artistry took place here at people's waists. Today, my vocation was slated to change. I was crossing over, and in a few felonious moments I would find out whether I had what it took to be a real road rat.

"Sounds like you got new shoes," Shep said in an effort to lighten the mood. This was about as tender as he could get. "Let me know when you think we've found the right corner," he told me, compounding my sense of inadequacy and dread. How was I supposed to know? Why couldn't he just take me to the place where all rats got started? Wasn't there a training ground for this kind of thing? Of course, the reason he left it up to me was because Shep, a good coach, was interested not only in finding out if my fingers were supple enough, but also whether or not fortune would smile on me. It's a process of autonomous triage that sets the pickers apart from the picked. Like dropping a line and waiting to see what bites, the object was to have me give it a try and, if unlucky my first time, admit that I was too small a fish to fry and let me get thrown back—in this case, to the tank. A few years in juvenile would season me for a more criminally-minded try next time. Except for one of his dozens of lucrative hustles, what did Shep have to lose but another greedy mouth to feed?

I was bent over like a sick man, bug eyes beholding portentous patterns in the poured concrete (bars, ball, chain, pair of powerful handcuffs, bed of bare springs). Grotesquely out of place on my unworthy feet: the sensational shoes. "How about we work here?" I blurted, without even taking a decent look around.

We had stopped at a nondescript corner near South Station: corporate buildings, broad sidewalks, and busy intersections.

"Nah." Shep said. "This corner's already being worked."

His characteristic clairvoyance served to resuscitate my inquisitiveness. Briefly distracted from my malaise, I said, "How can you tell?"

"How can I tell?" Shep said, tapping the toe of my sneaker with his red-tipped cane. "How *can't* you? There are a million indicators: a certain shift in atmospheric pressure, for one, the humidity level letting you know there's a rat in the area. Not to mention the speed of cheese shuffling over sidewalk and the wind of the picker whiffing . . . "

Just like Shep, making fun of me when I was most exposed. Burned by a blind man, I was really feeling badly now. I just wanted to get the initiation over with. It made no difference to me whether I failed or succeeded. Who cared if I ever kicked the nickname Eddie Feet? Introspection turned into bleak rumination, and Shep's cynical soliloquy was not helping.

". . . His nose scenting money in people's pockets. The taste of tin foil on his fingers . . ."

What did it matter if I could pick the pants right out of somebody's pocket and I got to be known as Something-Magnificent-Sounding Eddie? So what if instead I ended up trailing a string of luckless aliases in and out of juvie, jail, and the penitentiary for the rest of my life on account of a fumbled offense?

". . . Geese honking over Canada. The sound of a thousand far-off roller skates . . ."

I felt a fever coming on, and, like the explorer who decides to forget about building a campfire in the frozen face of an

Arctic gust because—yawn!—it would be so fine to just curl up and sleep, I was ready to be bundled off to a nice, cozy cell where I would have a good, long time to fend off the imminent hallucinations and cold sweats.

"How can I tell this corner's already being worked?" Shep still had not let up. "It's because *you* are the slippery-fingered sucker I smell coming a mile away even if I ain't blind *working* it!"

"What?" He had my attention now.

"And besides," he added as in afterthought, bending over and lowering dark glasses for an instant. Shep winked a bright blue orb right into the depths of my eye: "I ain't blind."

I was all pins and needles, overcome by awe and bewilderment, a mystic initiate with scales dropping from my glasses. Of course! Shep wore shades and carried a cane but he could see just fine. He was happy to perpetuate any masquerade that might help increase the take. Why had I never noticed what I saw now with perfect perspicacity? Hadn't Shep, especially in his gruff entreaties to action, always been so demure? He flashed a smile so disarming that, after an instant of ambivalence, I knew not to take it personally.

"Remember, Eddie," Shep went on, the shades replaced, his disability drama intact, already in progress, "crime is an art, and the criminal is an artist of disillusion." Holding his cane, facing the horizon, Shep gave the sidewalk a magic rap. I straightened right up. His terse pep talk had roused me and I forgot about my self-absorbed wallowing. I took a look around, found myself plopped right in front of the Federal Reserve bank, and right there, emerging like an augury from the revolving door, was my mark. He was running late, overweight, unkempt. Instead of scorn, derision, or pity, it was with gentle tenderness that I took in the slumped carriage, the stumbling gait, the henpecked perplexity, and the telltale, bulging pocket of a figure embossed by fate. My spirit soared. I had heretofore been crippled by anxiety over what I had believed would be duplicity. Indeed, if my motives had been insincere, then surely I should have succumbed to the attendant allergy known as self-incrimination, the symptoms of which had just gone into high-speed remission as my erroneous presumptions about thievery's misanthropy were instantly extinguished. In a flood of understanding, my sensibilities were saturated by a recognition of the art's essential altruism: The object was not to disdain those you steal from, but instead to take out of love. Tremendous tenderness is required to touch the mark, the pocket, the spirit. Without it, a rat will surely be trapped, and rightly so. Benevolent intentions are needed to buttress a taker's claim on borrowing a bit of society's scarce, scattered currency, that he might in turn tender a token of illumination. Hot coals of condescension were doused. The fire of fear fizzled out. Shame evaporated. I realized that pickpocketing was an extension of the very same ingenuousness I practiced as an illusionist. If it involved another hard-working Harry's cancellation of credit cards and acquisition of a little more scrip, these minor nuisances were more than offset by the magic involved in recognizing, for a moment, the relativity of his grasp on security, on reality, on the fragile spark of life that somehow takes so long to founder inside our tender breasts.

Like a salamander in my cool new shoes, I crept up behind the mark. It was as if a righteous, diabolical deity had reached down, mopped my brow, and moved me in a cosmic chess match, not just changing my place, but, by her touch, also my nature and shape. I went from illusionist to disillusionist, from pawn to rook or possibly bishop. Eddie Bishop, I considered for an instant. I liked that. At the moment of the snatch, an unswerving hand belonging to that god who guides businessmen and other thieves plunged purposefully from the heavens, parting the clouds like the seam of a pocket, and picked me.

Billy the Kid lasted less than a week. He moved on to another pack, went ward of the state, ended up at the bottom of the bay—we never really found out. What mattered to me was that, from the night he had named me, Billy's spontaneous exclamation had been a token of cheap if durable tin, a toy doubloon the other kids tossed around in callous afterthought which, over time, I would replace with real gold. Setting sleight of hand aside, I stuck with sticky fingers. It took months of persistent practice to change my nickname, bringing in the contents of ten, twenty, sometimes twenty-five pockets a day, never getting nabbed. Even Shep was impressed by my prowess. He said I spoke "el-o-quent-ly" about the elegance of the pick, and that I should lecture on the nuances of the art at school. Rats pestered me for my method and, insisting there was no secret, I instructed them in my simple provisions.

Lesson I: Lube

Some apply synthetic substances to the pads of the fingers, but when it comes to a pick, I believed in physiology's own educated intervention: natural lubricants. Long talons and luxurious locks were no longer the tools of my trade, yet I still had my active glands. Depending on the exigencies of the instant, the adrenal and pituitary systems provide uncut speed or morphine; thus does judicious collaboration between perspiration and salivation supply the necessary cocktail to whet fingertips for the grab. It's all about sweat and spit.

Lesson II: The Mark

There are the brutes who just goes for the suits, the psychologists who assemble impromptu personality profiles, and the superstitious pickers who select marks by cabalistic numerical sequences, but it really does not matter whom you pick. "Crime is an art," I told my apprentices, "and the criminal is an artist of disillusion. If we have to deceive and deprive to reach our audience, it is only so that the muse may make understood her charitable caprice." Talking points: not scorn, but sympathy; instead of misanthropy, altruism. By these means one determines who needs to be picked. Just as Robin Hood gave to the poor, so did he give to the rich. The gift: a sense of the vulnerability of all our amassed self-importance, abstract and material, and, subsequently, the nectar of ephemerality. The picker comes bearing a message of transience to be sent by special delivery.

Lesson III: Anonymity

Every road rat has to know to keep snout down. Ask any mark whether he got a good look at the suspect. If the pick was clean, what follows is a muddle of estimated height and shady hair color, yielding no nearer likeness for composite sketchers than that of your average kitchen broom. When the answer is yes, nine times out of ten the description begins with the eyes. Locking gazes with a mark is the first step to getting nabbed.

Whether or not other features are detected makes no difference compared to a connection with piercing pupils. These are the umlauts that define the ineffable letter, the capsized colon that begets incriminating testimony.

Lesson IV: The Dance

Some are transfixed by the details of the getaway: elaborate escape plans, decoys and relays, sizzling sprints. These thieves, by their compulsive precautions, end up begging pursuit, something a good picker never induces but for which he is always prepared. The primary object is to protect against any imperative for chase. All too often, however, a rat makes a mistake, in which case preparation can prevent disastrous capture. The answer is rarely an all-out sprint. When flight seems prudent, the getaway is better characterized as a ballet of picker, architecture, pedestrians, and traffic—the accursed cars and trucks that keep rats always on their toes. The job of escape is to detect the ebb and flow and spontaneously choreograph a dance to the urban score; the payoff is the getaway.

I have to admit that, no matter how many learned of the suppleness of my hands, a few of the kids from the early days never gave up on the name Eddie Feet. It was sort of cosmic justice, really, because, in a squeeze, when the mark got aware or a bystander beheld the take, it really did come down to—hold onto those spectacles—salvation's last resort: *Run!* The feet never failed, the shoes prevailed. Some rats attributed magical properties to my Nikes, the acquisition of which had marked a turning point in my career. As seasons passed and my lime sneakers turned the color of ripe avocado, they practically became a part of me. Sure, the shoes helped, but I knew I could do it without them, although the fact that I never stopped wearing the pair, whether in bed or bath, only stoked superstition. But it was just another habit, a pack precaution, like the way I kept my glasses on during sleep. In the rat world, the second you weren't using something it became free for someone else's scavengery.

After what seemed, over many months of expectancy, like an agonizing eternity to my juvenile eye, I observed a slow shift in nomenclature. At first, a few flattered me with Professor Eddie. Briefly, they teased with Eddie Fingers, then Eddie Frenetic, Easy Eddie, Wet Eddie—Eddie Anything, just so long as at the end of the day I brought in a batch of scratch. In the end, one name, my favorite, finally took. All over the city they spoke of the fleetness of Shep's fastest rat: Fast Eddie. That was me.

Long after my ascendancy, I remained restless in my guacamole specials. Winters came, summers went, and I knew I needed to go somewhere to find the answer to a pesky question. Year after year I kept up with the compulsion to lift leather, but despite my once-and-for-all liberation from guilty conscience, the job gradually took on a troublesome subtext. Of all the pockets I picked day after day, there was the chance that one of them might belong to someone related to me. Every strange face seemed to cry out, *Do I know you?* What if I ever pickpocketed Dad or pursesnatched Mom? The recurring nightmare: Peering into a purloined wallet at the detritus of another's life, I find a faded picture of an infant with moist forehead, familiar eyes, and huge blue booties. When any man in the world might be your father, any woman your mother, then no one can simply be your fellow. Everybody has shoes to fill, but there are none so large as the pair passed down by the unknown.

One summer day, a sooty sign at the Back Bay bus shelter caught my eye: a cartoon of a herdsman rubbing his stubbly chin, scrutinizing a lone lamb that had that wide-eyed, lost look. In place of a crook, the drover carried a neon question mark. Beneath the illustration, copy read: METZGER SHEPHERDING SERVICE. SPECIALISTS IN FILIAL IDENTIFICATION, CLAIMS, SETTLEMENTS. I decided it was time to figure out whether my question had an answer.

Left over on ancient Causeway Street, barely distinguishable between the ruins of the old highway and the yawning chasm of the abandoned tunnel, crouching in a perpetual penumbra cast by the skeleton of that hulking, indistinct monolith dubbed the Fleet Center, Metzger Shepherding was a brick blot on the city's history, one of the few offices remaining from the old North End. The building was probably already an anomaly, a relic of gaslights and two-lane streets, sometime halfway through century 20 when the viaducts had come and dwarfed it. Now, with the world's widest cable-stayed bridge eclipsing this part of the city like a monstrous wing and the tunnel's plugged mouth swallowing the neighborhood's light whole, the structure seemed doubly stunted. There in the dead heart of the city, beneath a peculiar pall of peace, I thought I heard a faint hum coming from the abandoned artery below.

I pushed the doorbell and stood under the scrutiny of the electric eye, sweating at the prospect of what I might discover, elated by the promise of release from beneath a long-amassed burden: a pocketful of money ostensibly my own. After pack dues and tributes to Shep, it had taken me too many seasons of squirreling away five-, ten-, and occasional twenty-dollar coins to save up the ten thousand weighing down my pants, half of it in change. I would be glad to give it away. After five minutes of unblinking surveillance and invisible deliberation, I was buzzed in.

An old man sat behind a great steel desk in the cheerless one-room office. His face was puckered like the butt of a lemon, his head as bald as the rind and his skin—from a long, lightless life in this hovel—just as jaundiced. He pointed to an empty chair. A few dusty calendars—all from different years, none of them current—drooped desolately from otherwise-unadorned walls. Long ago in this dingy little bunker, the man's enormous desk had been assembled like a ship in a bottle. Components that had barely squeezed through the door and been coupled before a remote war were all now thoroughly fused, nuts and bolts having long since rusted to oneness. The desk was in this room for good. It was the reason this building was still here, holding up leaky roof and fragile man alike.

"So," Señor Sourface said, noisily at work on one of those old hole-in-the-middle candies, "you think you can find yourself some honey, huh?" As if enveloping me in a cocoon of his confidence, the Metzger man—who by the looks of the cramped office served as owner, operator, and sole employee—leaned across a cluttered desktop plagued by a diaspora of last century's business: rogue pencils, vagrant paper clips, errant erasers, and a nomadic wrapper labeled "Pep-o-mint." Here in a brick box in the shadow of the now-silent overpass, that grimy, green steel landscape was something of a self-contained dimension, a barren expanse of office-supply apocalypse, the stray implements foraging for nourishment among scarce crumbs of efficiency. "Come on, cough it up. What's your angle, kid?"

Beady eyes betrayed callous calculations. Metzger Shepherding specialized in intimidating the rich with hearsay or trumped-up testimonies in order to exact settlements more accurately described as blackmail. There were enough bigamous bigwigs to bully around in the Beast who, however powerful, had fragile, family-values personae to protect and preferred paying the occasional extortionist in order to avoid paternity suits. It was not a new experience for me, coming up against a patronizing professional who had no time to waste on a delinquent kid. I had patted a lot of these guys from behind, but a face-to-face encounter required a different kind of skill and patience than hand-to-wallet. He had access to something that could not simply be lifted: information.

"Look, I'm not out to frame anybody," I said. "I genuinely want to know if you can tell me something about where I come from."

The patrimony policeman lowered his voice and, breath reeking of candy cane, delivered in grave tones what must have amounted to his standard, supercilious pitch. "You know, most of the sugar daddies who eventually settle don't even remember whether the claimant was an honest offspring, but they suck up the expense as a precaution, a symptom of their promiscuity, an annual inoculation for the health of their career." This said, he pepped up. "So, your mother's a whore, right? What's the name of the horny old lecher who sired you?"

Smarting, I said, "Honestly, I don't think either of them is alive."

My inquisitor's nose screwed up in revulsion. "You can't bribe a dead man."

"I just want to know what their names were, where they lived, whatever." I stacked the coins on the desktop. "I have the fee: five thousand dollars." Leaning over, he examined the pile, which seemed meager all of a sudden, and sniffed—not them, but me, perhaps to see if I, like leftover cheese, was off. I added a bit petulantly, "I've been saving an awfully long time."

"Saving? Ha!" he snorted. "More like stealing. Squandering someone else's hard-earned dough on your little vanity trip." Skeletal yellow fingers darted up from behind the desk, scooping the booty into a drawer. "You want me to believe you might be someone special, so you're holding out. Well, I've seen a million would-be Lindberghs."

I doubted that he had. This was the lowest of the birth brokers, a real cradle chaser, but his was probably the only office of its kind in town desperate enough to let a road rat in the door, and the service was within my price range. I figured that giving him the cash up front would at least compel Mr. Metzger (I presume; he never offered his name, nor a receipt for my chunk of change) to make cursory checks in hospital records and child-search networks.

He took my picture with an old-fashioned film camera,

my blood blot with a none-to-sterile-looking pin, and asked me whether I knew my birth date. "No. I'm not even certain of my age. Somewhere between twelve and fifteen, I believe."

"I'll run a search in the DNA databases to see if you were ever registered, but it's a shot in the dark," he said. "You sure you wouldn't rather keep the money and shoot up drugs or something?"

"How much time will you need?"

"I'll have your answer tomorrow afternoon, but if you ask me, you're wasting the dough. The chances of a rat like you finding an actual match are about as good as the Sox winning the pennant . . ."

I made my way to the door.

". . . the Pats taking the championship . . ."

I was back on the street and he was standing in the doorway, still going.

". . . the Celts coming back from the dead . . . the Bs taking the Stanley Cup . . ."

The next day, I delivered lunch to Shep's prescription booth and decided to tell him the news. I went into it feeling righteous. Going through the formal process was my idea of poignant passage: If there was a chance of finding relatives or the parents' final resting place, knowing as much before handing Shep the payoff might dilute my resolution to leave. Akin to the compulsion that had kept me aloft among power lines even after I had pretty much given up on getting the magic shoes, I held onto the superstition that an obstinate resolve might reward me with an aperture, however narrow, of hope.

Nervously fingering my eyeglasses, I said, "I had an interview with an agency."

"Agency, huh?" Shep said with full mouth, his words unintelligible to any but one of his most devoted rats, "Adoption or intelligence?" For Shep, I had procured a single five-thousand-dollar bill, obtained from a disdainful bank teller who had tallied up my coins with a disparaging glare. This was the apprentice's severance. Shep whiffed the fresh scratch stashed in the sandwich and plucked it from between pita and paper. He deposited the tribute in his pocket without acknowledgment and took a big, contemplative bite. Shep swallowed, chomped. "Because you need some smartening-up if you think the search is going to be worth it!"

I had expected a little railing. Shep did not let me down.

"A baby, you're thrown in the bull rushes," Shep began his harangue. "You float downstream, get plucked up by gypsies, make it to the head of the class, and end up leading your people out of the wilderness . . ."

For some time, Shep had perhaps sensed the imminent moving-on of one of his more rewarding rats. He had detected the remoteness in my voice and felt my mounting restlessness just as sure as he had heard the cache of coins accumulating in my pockets.

". . . or your mother dies giving birth—yours—and you never get a chance to kiss her proper, much less get a name besides *My baby!*, and so some goofball guardian ends up naming you alliteratively . . ."

I was beginning to feel like a shmuck. Shep had taken care of me since I was a tot; now I was repaying all those years of nurture with a slap of cold cash, as if all along he had been for hire like some kind of cabby.

". . . or you're sent off with a shepherd because of a really nasty rumor, but he's a sucker for your sweet feet, and he hands you to another flock-keeper who takes you away to grow up with a king and queen . . ."

Sheepishly, in an effort to derail Shep's derision, I said, "I recognize Moses and Nicholas Nickleby, but what about that last one?"

"It's from a play, one we don't get to 'til twelfth grade, so I guess you'll never know." I was ready to be getting on my way, tail between my legs, when Shep's expression was contorted by a venom visible even through obfuscating shades. "Best of luck, Eddie. Who's to say? Maybe there are a couple of fin-footed freaks out there on the lookout for their missing baby."

This one hit home. Shep's stinger bore a pernicious poison, and now I found myself fantasizing against all reason: What if my mom and dad could track me down, *had* tracked me down, just like that? Stupid stupid stupid. A sickening sunniness flooded my sinews. I wallowed in the septic warmth. Never before had I spoken this way myself, not even internally, but Shep, in his cosmic indifference, had given voice to a gut feeling that went all the way down into my tulip-bulb toes, the vibration of my desperate inner tone: Maybe *they* were trying to find *me*. This hapless wish ignited a little gas jet that had seethed in cool, odorless latency throughout my entire orphan infancy. Once you light a pilot like that, it never goes out.

"Well, Eddie," Shep said, "I hope you'll be one, big, flappy family."

A rage boiled up inside me. I saw things darkly. How could I have gone on so long with such a charmless child-user and a bevy of brothers who cared for nothing more than illicit gain? I kicked over Shep's stand and ran, leaving the make-believe blind man squawking maledictions and scrambling for his inventory. Shrieking with glee, a sink of rats from rival packs swarmed over the sidewalk and descended on the melee, making off with most of Shep's spectacles.

I walked alone through the streets of the Beast. Beyond the deserted aquarium complex on Central Wharf, black clouds of discord clustered out over the sea. Our Viking ancestors in their pagan-named ships: How had they dared sally so recklessly? At least Leif the Lucky had known whose son he was! Then those Protestants: their watery pilgrimage; their rock at Plymouth; the battles, suppers, and trysts with the Indians; their angry God and their scarlet letter; and, ringing across the years in modest saltboxes that served as churches, their story of a son who takes an advance on his inheritance, leaves home to go a-whoring, loses everything, ends up eating pig shit, and decides to come crawling back: His humility had been a luxury, his parable lost on rats without any dowry to squander, outcasts who would never know father, much less enjoy the option to bow before his mercy.

Stumbling unattached through throngs of button-pushers on break in the belly of the Beast, I brooded over the dumb mistake I had made. All those years without any knowledge of my origins, I had enjoyed all-you-can-eat illusions of imaginary parents. It was ridiculous to think there had ever been any chance of finding a biological family, and now I had alienated the only foster I had ever had. How would I get by without a daily dose of Shep's endearing indignation? Probably I would be crawling back by nightfall, having lost my dowry as well as seniority among the rats, ending up Eddie Feet again, made fun of more than ever before. Should I even bother returning to Metzger's office? The absurdity of the shepherding service enraged me. What would I get but a nope, no match, guffaw, I told you so, and a rubbing-it-in-my-face whiff of the fancy cigar the old man had bought with my front money; or at best the address of a cemetery where I could go look at gravestones? Shepherding! What had I been thinking? Read between the lines: delusions disabused—for a fee.

As a symptom of my malignant, advancing desolation, I had altogether lost the desire to pick. The million marks milling around the city did not incite the usual flair for helping others by helping myself. I no longer cared about them. Even if I did go and score a sack full of billfolds, wrapping myself in money belts like a gunner in holsters, who would there be to bring it home to? I had no Nec, no dough, no family. Why not give in, give up, turn myself over to the law? I had staggered across Columbus Park and all the way to Dock Square by the time I resigned myself to juvie, where at least I would get a plate of paste and a steel-picket place to dream about idyllic mom and dad and ruminate on how useless my descent had been.

In the lunchtime market throng, I spotted a cop on the stoop of Faneuil Hall, which over more than three centuries had witnessed a host of battles, both bloody and bilious. Mine would be an inconsequential defeat; I would go down anonymously.

I marched toward fate. Hands stuffed sheepishly into empty pockets, I must have seemed the apparition of an old-school gangster, striding purposefully with hidden pistols—and wasn't that what they were, after all, these legendary, offending weapons?—but really I was ready to flop over at the feet of the beady-eyed beagle, offering up empty fists to heavy-duty cuffs for which I, no longer a junior Houdini, held no concealed key. The constable, having caught notice of my approach, twirled his nightstick felicitously—much in the way,

I presaged, that the judge would wield his gavel at my hearing. I thought about how to word it so as to not waste too much of the badge cat's time: "Fast Eddie—maybe you've heard of me? Responsible for making thousands of pairs of pants a little lighter last year alone?" No, I did not deserve the patina of dignity, and anyway the O'Donnell might not believe me. Better to get the arrest over with and explain later at the station. Maybe: "Hey, shamus, your shoe's untied," then knee him in the eye. I was ten feet from a correctional destiny when I heard a voice remotely familiar.

"Hey! Those green sneaks!"

If years earlier he had seemed imposing in the slums of Beacon Hill at night, he looked even bigger now breathing down my neck at high noon in Quincy Market. Mano, the hacker I had left radiating in a Chevy like a rotisserie chicken, had finally caught up with me. He sported my orphaned Chuck Taylors, the uppers shredded almost to ribbons. Why had Mano kept these when he could afford any pair in the Beast? He must have had to stuff the toes with newspaper to force a fit.

The hulking hacker lurched towards me like a walking wall. Fuming fog from his nostrils, he snorted, "You're the son of a bitch who stole my Air Jordans!"

I took off over the bricks—a great upset of boxed lunches, an explosion of scavenger pigeons. Mano spirited after me, and the policeman, anticipating a good show, joined the chase. I sprinted east at North Market, ricocheted west at Quincy, then east again at South Market, but my pursuers knew all the convolutions. In the fury of my flight the glasses almost flew off my face. I wasn't sure I could outrun them. Mano was especially fleet for his size. He had spent his days training or at least, by the strategy of his trajectories, had been casing this area for a good long time. Had the jolt he received on Beacon Street endowed him with superhuman speed? West on State, site of the Beast's infamous massacre, I ducked into the old state house and scrambled up the corkscrew staircase, making a circuit under the dome and clambering back down in the wake of an irate docent, the dealer and the narc both hot on my heels.

"Wait up, Big Foot!" Mano said. I could feel his powerful huffing on the back of my neck. "There's something I've got to tell you." I knew better than to fall for that bully's trick. Doubling back down State I managed to lose the two momentarily, but given the trail of my big-bunioned pugs through this sooty neighborhood it seemed vain to hope for escape. I would not get out of this in one piece unless Mano got what he was after, but what could he want from me but blood?

Alarmingly, a burning spot shot through the heel of my right foot. It was unbearable, like a firebrand poking a hole through my sneaker. I sped up the steps of the Custom House, the great, granite temple that had gone from commercial center to luxury time-share to rave club before being converted into the Beast's water works. Hiding behind a column, I hastily unlaced, uncorking insufferable stench. I had not removed the shoe in many months. Off my foot it was like somebody else's severed limb, as nightmarish as a dumpster-dive run-in with a bio-bag. My bare sole, smoking slightly, felt instantly relieved, and deep inside the Nike I recognized the faintest coppery glint: It was One Cent come back to aid me in a jam! It had been so long since I had considered the cryptic token, and, while unconsciously I must have registered the absence, only now, with the coinstantaneous discovery of both its misplacement and its reappearance, did I detect a distant refrain of the fulsome song of fate. I found a chunk of broken glass and pried coin from insole, where it had been fused to rubber by ten thousand miles of pedestrian pressurization. It left a little impression of Lincoln. Abe's coppery face, tarnished from imbedded neglect, would take some fingering to make shine again. On the flip side, the monument had gotten brighter from constant polishing. Squatting beneath the Custom House portico, I scrutinized through my spectacles: After many months of getting rubbed, the person seated between the columns had become especially descript, and I was surer than ever that the two figures on the steps were people. In a wild surmise, I peeked around my pillar. Sure enough, two people were climbing the steps from opposite angles: Mano and the law's long arm.

I had expected lucky coins were meant to be used only once, but this one had come around recycled and its burning message was certain: Lose the shoes. It seemed to me like a reasonable ransom, although I wondered what anybody with eyes or a nose could want with those filthy sneaks. I pocketed One Cent, let the other high-top drop, and tossed the trusty pair in the air. Mano stopped in his tracks, gawked at the sky, and scrambled on a tangent across the stone steps. He couldn't have chosen a better pursuit angle. Mano tackled that badge cat with a *thwack!* and I booked down the stairs and past the tangled twosome to my barefoot getaway, leaving the linebacker to do the explaining.

Short of breath, satisfied that I had lost my stalkers, I

paused in front of Faneuil Hall to contemplate my fate. Full of adrenaline, invigorated by the chase, and reawakened to an old, doleful curiosity, I was suddenly satisfied to postpone self-sacrifice and pay a visit to Metzger Shepherding. If nothing else, perhaps the archaic autocrat would take a moment to explain to me what One Cent meant. Maybe he knew something about the picture on the tail. Clutching the coin, I set off on a barefoot pilgrimage.

By the time I got to Causeway Street I had almost lost my nerve. Standing at the threshold of the squat brick structure, I asked myself why I had come all this way. Strutting unshod across town at lunch hour had been a sure means, in my case, to generate humiliation. I might as well have let that lawman lock my legs in Faneuil Hall's historic stocks. Me and my silly One Cent! It was bad enough that Metzger was going to rip me off five thousand bucks, now I would also let him ride me for the worthless coin and laugh, just as half the people in the Beast already had, at my great, naked feet. Ringing the bell, I bleakly mused that the futility of the march did not matter. Once I came out, I would not have to walk all the way back to Government Center to find a cop to arrest me.

Metzger himself opened the door. "Eddie! Come in!" Not only did he call me by my name, he patted me on the back, and he didn't even wipe his hand afterward. Overnight his attitude had turned polite, practically solicitous. "Please, sit down." The patrimony broker leaned against the great, green desktop, now empty of clutter, and cleared his throat over and over. "Eddie," he uttered with a grave expression. An instant of clairvoyance told me there was news. I might get my dumb gravestones after all. Metzger was making an obvious effort to hold back emotion. If this was his damned-if-I-know spectacle, I decided it was worth five Gs just for the show. I would tell him this as a former performer myself. "Eddie. . ." he said. I leaned in close. "Eddie . . . Corrente!" he brayed. "That's your last name!"

The universe was boundless but in balance. There was nothing at its furthest reaches that could not be uncovered. There was a place somewhere that concealed the source, albeit decomposing, of my origins. I lay my head on that indestructible steel desk and pictured myself leaving One Cent at the site in a final act of expiation, then wandering the earth barefoot, ears deaf to common mockery. Afloat in a state of anaesthetized levity, I mumbled, "My mother and father—where are they buried?"

"Eddie, they're alive!"

Now I really felt sick. I had propped my parents' glowing, undefiled corpses affectionately atop my mind's pyre. Now Metzger, robbing me of that solace, threw a switch and reanimated them. They were out there, somewhere, stalking stiffly towards me with burnt-out eyes and outstretched arms. I had no control, at least not conscious, over my response: "Oh, no."

"They've been looking for you all these years and now they want to take care of you." Take care of me: What was that supposed to mean? It sounded like a Mafia threat or as if I was incontinent—either way you look at it, an awful arrangement. But what could I do? I had started this grievous process in motion and now I had to ride it out to the crash. Metzger had begun to brief me on the reunion, but I, in a daze, understood only that it involved going to Jersey. I was still reeling when I realized he was ushering me out the door. "Your ride is here."

At the curb, a stretch limousine. "Hold it . . . wait a sec . . ."

"Oh, by the way, here's your deposit back." Metzger handed me an envelope with a crisp five-thousand-dollar bill in it, not the tidy pile of coins I had stacked on his desk the day before.

"Deposit? What about the investigation, your contact commission—and what's this car about?"

"It's all taken care of," Metzger said, pushing me into the big, empty back seat.

"But—"

He shut the car door. "Been nice knowing you."

I fumbled with the buttons and managed to lower the automatic window, but, frowning like a disfavored dog, I didn't know what to say. Standing back on the curb, Metzger seemed relieved to be rid of me. And yet there was an aspect of dread in his retreating figure that seemed to imply the possibility—and at once, with my lame luck, presage the certainty—of our future meeting. "Good luck," he called, "son." Son, he said. It was the first time anybody had ever called me that, and instinctively I was repulsed. If someone had to do it, why did it have to come so patronizingly, in such dispiriting circumstances, from this shyster's simpering lip? It struck me as so premature and abrupt that I instantly, internally rejected the designation like a transplanted kidney of the wrong blood type.

What might have been excited anticipation was

contaminated by a sense of entrapment—echoing in my head: *They want to take care of you*—capped off by the limousine imprisonment, tinted glass between front and back keeping me from seeing who was at the wheel. I was awakened to the awful claustrophobia of the situation: I was confined to a back seat, and it might as well have been in a squad car—after all, it was a car. To think that just an hour before I had almost been overcome by the impulse to surrender! I could barely buttress the metaphysical gravity. These were the very vehicles that haunted rats on our runs. They were the predators of the street, always out to take us down. Not a few rats had gotten popped and been forced to spend weeks recouping, months catching up with missed rent. Being shut in a box is something you never get used to and yet, with practice, you can train yourself to access that smidgen of cool. The limo captivity unlocked the old escape artist within. I knew better than to bang on windows or shoulder the door and roll. To forestall hyperventilation, I summoned my old deep-breathing techniques. I had enough oxygen to last indefinitely, there was no external menace (sword, saw, shark). In fact, the only exigency was at my bladder. Sometimes the best means of escape is to wait.

There was a certain novelty to the luxury: a fridge full of drinks, a telephone, a TV with virtual reality. But I already had to pee. Who would I call? And I was too busy watching the world go by—fast!—to stare at a screen. Ever since those underground stretches of I-93 and the Pike had been abandoned, navigating a car around the Beast meant a royal snarl, but things sure sped up out on 95 South. Too timid even to tap, much less ask the driver to stop for a bathroom break, I rolled up the five-G note Metzger had pressed on me and, disowning the tender that had gotten me into this fix, stuck it in the back seat ashtray for the ghost chauffeur's gratuity. One Cent in my pocket was all I had left. In the rush, I never had gotten a chance to show the old codger the coin.

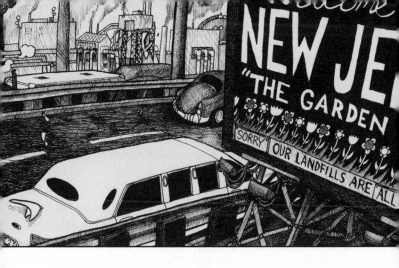

Overnight it was all over. It was that simple. The wondering was done with just for the asking. Then the questions began coming even more furiously than before: they kept asking me until I was worn out with words. Had it been a mix-up at the hospital? An aborted kidnapping? A black-market sale? Had they lost me on the tyke ride at the state fair? "Corrente"— could be Roman, Egyptian, Akhaian . . . you name it. It sounded European, but it might have just as easily been Middle Eastern or African—you could never be sure, the area around the Mediterranean turning so murky, ethnically, with rivers running north, occupations every which way, and King Ptolemy back in the day letting all the brides get switched, swapped, and swiped. Was there a place known as Correnth somewhere? Could it have something to do with humans evolving out of an ape named Cornelius? "Eddie Corrente"—

kind of rhymed, a little alliterative. Perhaps I had descended from an old-world werewolf: part man, part jackal. That would explain my drawn-out dew claws. Maybe my freakish feet were the product of a sorcerer's art, an unnatural graft: the embellishment of man's frame with falcon talon or baboon paw. I guessed I had the sort of name privileged kids made fun of in school. I supposed I would find out.

It was a long ride, but I managed to distract myself from urologic urgency by concentrating on the surrealistic scenes flashing by on road signs. When the highways had been privatized, junction, exit, and speed limit markers had been turned into unjuried art spaces. Graffiti were the preferred media by which packs and posses competed for unofficial posts as poet laureates. Gradually mesmerized, ultimately exhausted, I bounced around half asleep in the back seat, monotonously hallucinating sparkling urinals and snapping to just before allowing myself to take a leak.

When the driver took the first Jersey exit I started to feel ill at ease. The fresh air caused me to cough and the smells of nature got me queasy. All that nauseating verdure made me sweat. The car turned left onto a smooth, clean street that looked like a flat from a movie set, with grand houses set far back on broad lawns shaded by monstrous trees. Back in the early 2000s, before TV had become interactive, there had been a weird phenomenon called the situation comedy. People would sit down for thirty minutes and watch an awful stew of generic jokes, romantic drivel, and canned laugh tracks. These domestic grotesques, set mostly in horribly bright living rooms with windows onto overgrown foliage, had been shot on this same green street—I was sure of it.

When the limo pulled up to the curb I could barely see out the windows: There was a geared-up photographer jockeying for position on one side and two frightening, flattened faces pressed against the glass on the other. My door opened and I stepped from the back seat with no sense of modesty, never once having had the occasion to emerge from a car of any kind. Bleary, bladder filled to bursting, heart pounding, pores pouring, I was showing it all to the world, as they say, except in my case that meant a pair of rare, bare feet.

"Well, will you look at that, Daddy!" she started things off. "He's got loaves like you got dough."

"Now, now, Mother," his first chirp, "mustn't tease junior."

She was busty. He had a belly. They were well-to-do political types, the mayor of Ho-Ho-Kus and his gung-ho wife. Cheerful, liberal, Universalists, chummy names: Pauly and Merry. "That's M-E-R-R-Y. People ask me, 'As in the Mother of God?' And I say, 'Nah, like Christmas!'" They thanked God and said they hoped I did too—however I might imagine him or her. I supposed that I resembled them as well as I could anybody, although their shoe sizes were clearly single-digit.

The first thing I said addressed what everyone, including the gawking photographer, his jaw dangling low like the camera bags slung from his shoulders, was looking at: my feet, between which I compulsively shuffled. "Honest," I tried, head down, already contrite, "they're my only excess."

Merry said, "Can't wait to see."

"Say again?" Pauly said.

"I said you need to pee, honey? It's a long haul from Baltimore."

"Not Maryland, Mother. They found our boy in Mass."

"Sure," she said to nobody in particular, with a wink at me.

We all three froze in place to let the photographer take a pict. I wasn't sure if I instinctively, genetically, knew what to do or if the parents' already-iron hold was manifesting itself tele-kinetically, but even without explicit prompting I mugged like the best of them. Pauly yoked a hairy arm across my shoulder. "Jeez," he said, "your clothes are soaked. Was the sunroof open? Cloudbursts over Connecticut?"

Inside the house, the head was a nightmare right out of Dr. Seuss. Everything I touched—pristine porcelain, gleaming steel, glowing terry cloth—was instantly sullied. Although aghast at the marks I had made, what I saw when I emerged into the kitchen more than compensated for my shame. The alien grown-ups nonchalantly proffered a wagon wheel of a pizza: thirty-six inches in diameter, extra cheese and sauce, the works. Convinced that at any moment I might awaken and find that pie, if not parents, had turned out to be just part of a dream picnic, I dispensed with all modesty and wolfed five slices. Mama picked off the anchovies and could not finish even half a piece. Pops put away a couple but left his crusts. I had not inherited their meager appetites. When the folks pushed their plates away, I obliged by taking care of the scraps.

After the meal, Pauly and Merry drove me up broad, carpeted stairs. At the top, they showed me my room. "Your" and "room" sounded absurd in the context, especially together. That's when I realized: These affable freaks really mean it. The huge bed was covered with fluffy wadding that sank a good foot when I sat on it. There was a chest neatly brimming with folded clothing, packages of clean briefs, and new tube socks, extra-long. The magnanimous padrón said he would send out for any brand of sports shoe I wanted, and when instinctively I said, "Converse!" I thought I detected a disapproving grimace. I held to the consolation of my first-pair brand with a desperate clutch, as the shipwreck victim bobbing in spin drift hangs onto the sole, floating coconut.

In the living room, I sat up straight and very still in my grimy, tattered shirt and pants, certain that by the slightest movement I would soil the snowy cushions of the poofy armchair. Pauly and Merry cradled cocktails on either end of the couch and spoke remotely of their "journey" to find me, a battle of hope and courage. The tale was not very specific, but full of heroic rhetoric. It sounded like they had already told it to a TV crew or two. When the time rolled around and Pauly turned on the late edition of the local news, it turned out they had. It was the lead story. They absorbed the report without comment. After it was over, Pauly said to himself with some satisfaction, "I sound downright senatorial when I say 'ordeal.'" Merry commented on the look of the lawn.

Over his second drink, Pauly delivered a little speech. "I'm the guy who privatized the sewage industry. The operating system for all the formerly-public works in the Northeast— that was designed by yours truly. When I was a youngster like you, the Internet was bringing anything and everything to your door faster and easier than a phone call. I said to myself, you can get the Net to deliver media, groceries, and consumer goods to the average American home, but what about what they want to have taken away? And then it hit me," Pauly said, wagging a finger over his head to represent that old light bulb glowing, "—shit! They'll never be able to break down piss and shit into bytes and bits." Pauly carried a big bankroll in his pocket.

By the bulge, I would say a tidy hundred grand in a fat, gold clip.

Shyly, I said, "Um, any idea how I got these feet?"

"Grandmaternal influence," Pauly grumbled. "Recessive trait, you know. You should have seen the dogs on that lady! Yup—you're a dead ringer for the face, too!"

"Do you have any pictures?"

"We used to have albums full, but they were all lost."

"How?"

"Fire," Merry sputtered, while simultaneously Pauly spewed, "Flood!"

"Uh, it was a fire flood," Merry corrected herself, "the kind that fires up on you all of a sudden. Isn't that right, Daddy?"

"No, Mother. You're always mixing that up. Flash flood."

"Sure, how silly of me. The Passaic just kept rising over the riverbanks. Remember, Daddy?"

"Hackensack, Mother," Pauly said, his eyes narrowing. "It was the Hackensack River."

"Hackensack. Sure."

"Seems like you're getting kind of tired, Mother. Why don't you let the boy and me have a little man-to-man?"

"Sure, Daddy," Merry said, rising. Laying a warm, fragrant hand briefly on my cheek, she added, "Sweet dreams, handsome!"

After fixing himself another cocktail, Pauly went into a little more detail about the split of our stories. "Merry and I were teenage sweethearts. We got started early, and boy was it fun to . . . to find out we were going to have a child. Trouble is, she did it kind of young. This was before my lucky break, and her father thought I was a good-for-nothing, so he took you to an orphanage. Somehow, from there, you ended up a derel—er, street kid. The old man kept the trail a secret, but he sure didn't count on me striking it rich after he kicked the bucket and managing to track you down." Pauly finished his drink with a snort.

"Um, Dad," I said. After a momentary lapse he squinted at me, seeming as irritated by his new appellation as I was by mine. "I forgot to ask back at the agency—what was my given name?"

"Your given name?"

"As a baby. What did you call me?"

Pauly fidgeted with his swizzle stick, eyes darting nervously between glass and floor. I figured it was just the standard shiftiness that comes with being a politician, compounded by the weirdness of meeting his kid after all these years. His expression a little pickled, Pauly blurted, "Eddie, of course."

"That's funny."

"What?"

"Well, considering that's what my pack master—guardian, I mean—named me too, completely independently."

"He didn't know anyone at the orphanage?"

"Nope. At least not according to his story."

"What a coincidence. Well, I sure am beat. I better get to bed. Good night, son." There it was—that terrible word again!

Upstairs in the silent house, I peeled off the ratty shirt and pants that had kept me self-conscious the entire evening and, after removing my one possession from the pocket, deposited the grubby clothes in the trash. Attached to my bedroom was a private bathroom. Instead of the hole in the boards in the basement of the Nec, there was a bright, white throne. When I flushed, I thought of Pauly's cash register ringing. I reclined for more than an hour in the polished trough, in awe of the efficacy of suburban plumbing, filling and refilling with hot water a casket-like conveyance I knew, from picts on the Net, to be a tub. Soap bubbles disintegrated on contact with my skin. I made a gray halo just below the rim. The way the street had built up layers on me, I would have left a ring around Lake Michigan.

Although I was not accustomed to changing clothes, least of all before turning in, I buttoned up in flannel pajamas Merry had laid out on my pillow. Climbing into the sack felt strange, like wearing shirt and pants for a swim, and bare feet in bed felt even weirder. The long soak had not rinsed away the smell of the city and I was all too full of bravura for the fresh, clean sheets. I feared the odor of the streets would so soak the stuffing that my redolence would never dissipate, even if by morning my pristine parents had to throw out the mattress. I removed my glasses and placed them atop the bedside table, glancing briefly, blurrily, leerily at the profile of Lincoln. While the coin's discovery had gotten me out of binds twice before, the steps at which it had intervened had succeeded, in the long run, only in depositing me here in Ho-Ho-Kus, and I wasn't sure I liked it. Scrubbed, exhausted, dropping off to sleep, I considered this token from the life I had left behind. What did Abe, with his unpredictable devices, have in store for us?

Everything was so bright and white I thought I was dead. In the canyon-deep streets of the abandoned factory district off Kendall Square, which most of the day lolled in the wan reflection of urban brick, our nearest star rarely peeked over the roofs until noon, even in summer's bloom. But the windows of my new bedroom faced east, right into the rising sun. The mattress had proved cripplingly supple. I was bent and arthritic from just one night in all the fluff, and I had soaked the sheets with sweat. This would not have seemed unusual, except that it had happened as the result of a dream. I never dreamed. Other rats who lived ulterior lives at night, sustaining themselves on secret, somnolent identities as sports stars and pack masters, had tried to convince me that I dreamed like all the rest, only did not remember. Yet I was adamant. I never dreamt. I slept deeply, somewhat peacefully. But, if anything, I had used up all the REM watching my all-absorbing question roll by. I supposed that it was only natural to now redeem the repository of dreams, as the day before I had obtained a dramatic, specific, and somewhat dreary answer. *Where do I come from?* had all of a sudden become *Here*. In lieu of the exhausted question, Morpheus had at last bestowed upon me my first nocturnal adventure.

It had actually been a series of dreams, all with the same unspectacular, pedestrian theme: running, running, running . . . from drug dealers . . . from a thousand pocket-picked plaintiffs . . . from an overzealous orphan broker . . . from Shep and the rest of the Nec . . . These had all been pretty standard shrift, the kind of chases I generally enjoyed. What turned dream into nightmare was the dash that, at last, I stood to lose, away from pursuers who were gradually, grievously gaining on me: mush-mouthed mom; doting, dipsomaniac dad—both hopelessly, horribly middle-class. Certainly, I was chagrined by my first flight of midnight fancy. If that was all there was, an exhausting extension of the dull grind of day, then I decided I could do without the dreaming of dreams. I got up, unbent myself, peeled off damp pajamas, toweled dry, and prepared for the descent into my first big day as somebody's son.

Dressing, I wistfully regarded the forlorn heap of clothing I had left in the trash. Feeling oppressed by all the stiff elasticity although sporting only shorts and socks, I wished I could climb back into my comfortable old rags. Still, I would oblige the proud parents with clean, creased clothes. Was that not the minimum a kid could do? I selected a green sweatshirt (Go Jets!) and a too-crisp pair of jeans from the chest. Back in the Beast, I never would have been caught dead in fresh denim.

The fit made me think of stuffing my legs into mailing tubes, wrapping a stovepipe around my rear. The only thing that saved the pants was a feature sewn into the top of the right pocket: a trim, additional pouch, perfect for concealing a small amulet. I picked up One Cent from the bedside table. Considering my options—slipping it between layers of bed, flipping it into the back of a drawer, dropping it in the toilet and disposing of it with a vigorous flush—I frowned and asked for some sign. *Are you lucky?* Naturally, that question was for myself as much as for my miniature mascot, but no matter how I glared he would not look me in the eye. Sure, I could have compelled him to talk: heads, yes; tails, no. But that would have forced an ultimatum for which neither one of us, perhaps, was prepared. As it appeared I would have to wait for a definitive indication, I ended up reluctantly depositing the old profiled president snugly into my new, blue demi-pocket. I took one last look in the mirror on the back of the bathroom door: big, blanched feet, regal jeans, Lincoln green. At least by wearing the outfit I would not have to look at it.

Pauly had already left for work and Merry was not yet awake. Padding around in stockinged feet, I took the opportunity to privately survey the ground floor, beginning with wood-paneled study: desk, shelves, ottoman, an obtrusive exercise machine, and the most unusual furnishing, situated conspicuously in front of the desktop term, an antique commode. I surmised that it functioned, as the bowl was bolted to the floor and there was water inside. This must be where Pauly got his work done. Lining the walls was a broad collection of those big, clumsy artifacts: books made from paper, novels and the like. I wondered which parent had read them. By the light of the living room shag, I took inventory of all the uncomfortable furniture that was supposed to make a home. On the glass-brick bar, a golden trophy held a couple of teeny toothpicks while the littlest egg cup burst with a garish bouquet of the old man's souvenir swizzle sticks, no two the same: among them a busty rumba dancer, a mini–model jet, and a blue sheep that read "A gift from . . ." and bore the long name of the Greek ambassador to the UN. Lining the edges of the dining room's terra cotta, cabinets were stocked with privets, cozies, caddies, and coasters of all kinds, along with an eclectic flotilla of containers: six-ounce tea cups to ten-gallon lobster pots and a great array of in-between goblets and crocks. At the back threshold was that kind of chamber peculiar to the rural home: The immediacy of outdoors composed not only of steel and stone yielded the mandate of a mud room, with bare wood furnishings and polish-stripped fixtures for sloughing off soil.

I felt a little uneasy sliding across kitchen linoleum. The room was way too bright, all glass, steel, and white Formica brimming with bottles, canisters, and cardboard packages bathed in buttery sunlight, but a dozen assorted donuts on the table quelled my malaise. I sat down with them before the news term, which carried a page-one pict of my parents and me with the caption: "Native Son Returns to Ho-Ho-Kus!" Mercifully, my feet had been cropped.

I had set to work on the dough, hitting my stride at nut number ten, when Merry came down, still in her nightgown. She stood blinking in the doorway with beautiful bare knees and a bold V-neck cleave, squinting at me like something alien and unfamiliar, frowning to remind herself what had happened the previous evening.

"Gawd! I didn't know you'd be up already, honey! Don't I look a mess?"

She staggered blindly in front of the bright window and through the sheer fabric of her nightie I got a glimpse of bulging owl eyes. I averted my gaze to her fuzzy slippers. She had sweet little feet. It was a wonder what had come out of her. Merry shuffled her way to the coffee machine, groped for the pot, and poured. She sat across from me and plunged into her mug, resurfacing a moment to mutter, "It's the first day of your new life. Shouldn't you be sleeping 'til noon or something?"

"I always get up early. Besides, I'm not used to the sun."

"Did they keep you in a dungeon or something?" she muttered from the dark-roasted depths. "Anyway, your new clothes look nice." Merry's eyes started to shine as the bean worked its mojo. She placed the steaming cup on the table and lay a hot, soft hand on the back of my neck. "We have so much to catch up on, Ed."

My eyes at the level of her swelling chest, nose trapped by the dilation of her heaving cleavage, I fiddled nervously with the bridge of my glasses and mumbled, "Please, I prefer— *muh!*" She clutched my head in both hands and pressed it between her breasts. A cocktail of convoluted passion stirred inside me. My mouth watered. My tongue ached with a dull longing. I was all choked up. I felt my lips swelling. I guessed it was for love of mother, but I could not be sure. Was this the way sons were supposed to feel? My head was spinning, thoughts were swimming. A drunken distraction overtook me. Just when I thought I couldn't take any more the air was filled with bells. It was a clanging from on high, a cosmic disclaimer, the clamor of a deity's disfavor. As the tolling subsided, in a flood of emotion I grabbed Merry back. "What was that?"

Before I realized that she had even let go, Merry turned her back and was ferrying her coffee away. My lenses were foggy and smudged. "See who's at the door, honey," she said nonchalantly. "I'm not dressed."

On the stoop, a brown-suited courier came bearing a parcel. It was a good-looking package, the kind I might have swiped had I seen it at the station out of range of someone's grasp. "Mister Corrente?"

"He's not here."

"I have a delivery for a Mr. Edward Corrente."

"Oh. The name's Eddie."

"Sign here." He handed me a pad. Barely recovered from the doorbell racket, still reeling from mammilary knowledge of Merry, here I was with my third big shock in as little as a minute. Sure, I knew how to write what he wanted, but should I assume the new nomenclature just because the so-called shepherd who had sampled my DNA told me to? Over the past twelve hours I had entertained answering to Eddie Corrente, but that was very different from inscribing myself such. Although admittedly I had not consciously considered bailing out, thus far it had all felt like a free trial, no obligation to buy. But the way these things worked, the digital signature would go into a database with a billion other declarative John Hancocks. If I cast this assumed identity in cyberstone, didn't that presume embodying this new Jersey personality for virtual eternity? Could I so brashly define myself as my every mother's son, my daddy's little girl? I was on the adrenaline edge, tearing myself in two between fight and flight, when the delivery man added, "An X will do."

Inside the box, wrapped in wispy tissue: the most grotesque pair of footwear I had ever seen. It took four different shades and grains of cowhide just to mold the toes, and the clashes continued on up the sides in all the hues of a Technicolor yawn. Even the laces made a multicolor zigzag pattern. It was hard to believe they were Cons, but there it was on each of the tongues: the trademark star.

"Bring them inside!" Merry roared from the hall. Doomed, I did. "They're huge—those things would probably even have fit Pauly's mom! Well, go ahead, Ed. Put 'em on!" I swallowed and slipped the hideous things over my socks. To my dismay, they fit. "Why don't you take a stroll around the block?" Merry said. "Break 'em in."

I was Frankenstein tromping down the street. The neighborhood's extravagant houses were like layer cakes behind the bullet-proof glass of a bakery that the day before would have refused to buzz me in. The shoes were awful. With each step, a sickly anaesthesia seeped into toes, arches, heels, heart. The shells themselves were light, but dragged on my spirit like lead, the feeling worse than when feet fall asleep. It was like lugging around a couple of dead, wet cats.

As I returned to my new trap, a pall of gray descended and rain began pelting me. The shower seemed to bode well, reminding me of the distant comfort of urban shadow, and perked me up a little when I went back inside. From somewhere on the ground floor came a deafening whine like the howls emerging out of the underground of a rat's faraway yesterday: the hydraulics of the T careening around subterranean curves, the moan of air-conditioning exhaust from the sidewalk vent of a South Station skyscraper, the echoing hollers of a Dig City rally. Dwellers of the street always detected such speech right under their feet, and I was drawn to the source of the comforting cacophony. But how had these urban strains harkened their way here? Overcome by a combination of infantile impulses—exhilaration, disorientation, even a little dependency—voice cracking, I called, "Mom?"

"In here, honey!" she shouted cheerfully over the hypnotic dissonance. I walked into the living room, face flushed with anticipation and a zeal to please. Merry had nosed herself and the vacuum cleaner into the far corner of a field of immaculate white. Approaching, I thought I'd ask if I could help. Merry raised her eyes to me, her own countenance flooded with affection that would seem sufficient to bring me to my knees. Bent over to get beneath a table, the full furlough of her chest beckoned pendularly. In my mind, I did not resist. Merry lowered her gaze and her complexion turned ashen. O gawd! had she caught me looking at her tits? Overwhelmed by feelings at once arousing and unpleasant, those of both infant and man, I turned away. That's when I saw the trail in my wake. Huge treads had tracked mud all over Merry's clean carpets. With the irrational inkling that it might undo the damage, I made haste to retrace my steps, resulting in a calamitous run-in with an end table. One of my two left feet glanced off a delicate wooden leg, triggering a chain-reaction of crystal figurines and porcelain notions, after which the hip pocket of my dungarees hooked the corner of the sideboard, setting off another avalanche. By the time the fiasco was finished, my reeling heels had upset the populations of practically all the living room's surfaces and the white carpet was covered with the black schematic of a bizarre tango.

Merry did not get angry. She would not indulge me with the kind of hostility I was used to as a rat. Instead, she cooed from the kitchen, "How about a nice mug of hot cocoa? Mommy makes the best hot cocoa." Flushed, sulking, defeated by toppling furniture and traitorous trinkets, I sullenly sipped at the bitter, scorching liquid, knees and hips mottled black-and-blue beneath the denim of new jeans.

Cursing clumsy feet and convulsing hip, which together threatened to imperil the tenuous filial bond, I spent the rest of the day where I could not hurt anybody or anything: in the study, on the recliner, with my shoes up where I could see them. Bound volumes with suspiciously uniform spines all shelved at attention, the Corrente family editions, when quarried for their contents, answered my roll call with martial decorum, one by one barking *crack!* Desperate for consolation, I turned to Melville and the nostalgia of those terrestrial passages set around my erstwhile home state, the sibling tenderness of Ishmael's surprise at finding himself in bed with Queequeg, and a seafarer's empathy for the sense of inescapable alienation.

Merry interrupted "The Counterpane." "I made you a sub for lunch, honey. Mommy's got some special shopping to do, and when Daddy and I get home we'll have a special treat."

"Have you read any of these?"

"Nah, Daddy bought 'em by the yard. Pauly plays with his computer and I use this room to work out, but a mayor's supposed to have books." She shrugged. "By the way, what's 'Moby' mean?"

"I'm not sure. Large, I think. Or maybe immortal."

"Wow. What's it about?"

"A really big fish."

"Too bad."

I looked forward to Pauly getting home that first night, if only for remission of how mortified I felt at being left alone with Merry. Maybe he could help salvage this day for me. Perhaps I still stood a chance to make a reasonably healthy start in my new life. Bored by "Cetology," I fingered Pauly's term awake, closed the lid on the commode, and took a seat in front of the screen. By the books, I could see he wasn't kidding about the fortune, but the rest had been braggadocio. It was written all over Pauly's emails: I was a son of a plumber. In 1643, Italian mathematician and physicist Evangelista Torricelli had discovered the basic principle behind water pressure systems. Some four centuries later, Pauly Corrente, crouched inside a cabinet with pants at half-mast, ass smiling vertically into the kitchen, bumped his head on a P trap and got a bright idea. Pauly found a couple of computer geeks to program the code and, early on in the Age of Deregulation, when so many bankrupt cities sold off control of their utilities, he bought up the water works and began making billions as a plumbing racketeer. The simpleton genius at the heart of his plan: If a city didn't pay, he could make it so waste never went away. *We're sorry . . . try your flush again later.* After reading all about it, I did not picture myself as a legacy of sepsis, but if nothing else I got the idea that, with a little imagination, any loser could do better than remain a sideshow act all his life.

I ate Merry's hoagie and went wearily up to my too-bright room. Hallucinations of a phantom hand broke up my fitful nap, and I was roused from shallow sleep to the waking nightmare by that abominable sound: "Son?"

Half-awake, disoriented, I stumbled to the door. "Surprise!" The Correntes stood at the bottom of the stairs, Pauly burdened with bundles, Merry holding a flaming cake. Just my luck: I had found my parents on the eve of my birthday. After putting out the fire, I uneasily ate an obligatory piece of saccharine sponge. Surveying my feet approvingly, Pauly said, "Nice shoes."

I already felt weak, and yet it was time to unwrap the gifts: a skateboard the size of Manhattan, huge snowshoes or two oversized tennis rackets, and a whole host of spherical missiles in a variety of sizes and shapes, from base and basket all the way to foot. Merry had already begun stashing this stuff in the hall closet when Pauly held out a small box. It looked harmless, hardly larger than his hand, and he seemed so eager to foist it on me that I plumbed a last reserve of fortitude. While the ribbon slithered to the floor, Merry and Pauly, each duly coiled, prepared to pounce. The lid popped off of its own accord. On a little bed of cotton wadding lay something altogether too familiar that, in the context of a gift, appeared before me as a ritualistic object of dread. "Mother helped pick it out," Pauly said.

I must have blanched when I lifted it like a dead thing with trembling fingers. "A wallet." I parted the pockmarked cowhide. Folded inside was a crisp, parchment-proof ten-thousand-dollar bill. The ink was as green and bright as an emerald. Merry squealed with delight.

"Here's another little item to put in it." Pauly palmed something from his coat pocket. "Close your eyes and put out your hand."

I immediately knew what it was by the touch. "I haven't taken a test," I protested.

"Sure, but I know some nice guys down at motor vehicles. I take care of their parking tickets; they take care of the little incidentals."

"But I don't even know how."

"Aw, it's easy, honey," Merry said. "I taught myself in a day."

"Best way to learn," Pauly chimed in. "Besides, you won't have to worry about getting pulled over in my town."

The license contained rough estimates of my height and weight, erroneous data about hair and eye color, and the DOB allowed me for the first time to calculate exact age. "I'm seventeen?"

"Sixteen, really," Pauly said, "but we added a year so you can go it alone."

The pict had been lifted from the news story on the Net. The text read "Edward P. Corrente," doubly upsetting, for the formal first name and the surly sur-. "Wait—what's the 'P' for?"

"We thought you might like it . . ." Merry began.

"And if you want, you can even start to go by it," Pauly added. "A lot of great men have gone by middle names, you know," he pontificated, as if someone should have been taking dictation, "F. Scott Fitzgerald, O. Henry . . ."

"It wasn't there in the first place," Merry ran on, "but we figured we would put it in since we had to get you a birth certificate."

"Because of the flood," Pauly said.

"Sure," Merry corroborated, "flash flood."

"Of course, we can't simply call you Pauly, that's already taken. And plain Paul would be confusing, you being the younger and everything."

An uncertain admixture of horror, repulsion, and scorn welled up in me. There wasn't any definite target for the volatile combination—after all, the folks just thought they were being nice. Merry drove home the poisonous spike: "Pauly Junior, though—that has a nice ring."

I was led outside in a demented daze. In the driveway, there was a brand new SUV with a big bow on top. Pauly jangled the keys in front of me. It took a mammoth effort of will to get my lips to part. My slightest movement was stifled, as if the world had been submerged in honey, and the words came out like bubbles. "I can't tell you how strongly I feel. I think I have to lie down for a while."

Merry pouted. "Aw, aren't you hungry, PJ? Daddy and I were going to take you out to dinner."

"I'll get something from the kitchen," I lied. As a matter of fact, with my first taste of the cake, drenched with signification, my inexorable appetite had been misplaced. "And would you mind calling me Ed—"

"No problem, Ed," Pauly interrupted.

"—*dee*. Please, Ed-dee. Just call me Eddie."

I wobbled back upstairs on unsteady legs. I was sixteen, same as my shoe. I hoped that they—age and size—would not continue to increase in tandem. Before shutting the door to my room, I heard Merry say, "Did you see how surprised, Daddy?"

Pauly replied, "Just like your mother, Mother."

Pickpocket is picked off the street and plopped smack in the cleave of comfort's bosom, goes from nesting in newspapers to getting engulfed by a gaggle of goose down, from barely paying the rent to having a bomb of an allowance, from wearing out cheap cloth sneaks to crushing concrete in calfskin slam-dunkers. I should have been happy, right? On the contrary, something about meeting my parents germinated a bleak delinquency that summer caused to bloom into full-fledged dementia. It festered while I lay awake at night, my imagination returning to the soporific sounds of train brakes, jet engines, and truck axles rattling over fretted Kendall roads. I longed for the reassuring trickle of leaky pipes, the uplifting blast of a broken window's cold draft, the comfort of a newspaper cot.

A kid is supposed to take a decade and a half to enjoy the laid-back buffet, a smörgåsbord of dolls and toy trucks, of going out for teams, trying on different styles, and getting rejected for dates, but I, after an abortive infancy, had been required to rush straight into adulthood. After all those years of callused self-sufficiency, I found myself cracking the can and getting to the contents of the teen inside. He had been there all along, hibernating like a locust. As a juvenile criminal, I had been the goody-two-shoes, a sweet boy, obedient and idealistic. Now, as a town-and-country kid, I felt as if incarcerated, high-top shoes laced over my ankles like leg irons, a literal chain, the wallet's bane, around my waist.

As for the SUV, I refused to pilot that metal death monstrosity. It sat in the driveway, the bow still on the hood. And so, as I walked everywhere, I had to wear the horrible high-tops. When I had requested Cons, the options in my imagination had been limited to flimsy, synthetic, and monochromatic. How I pined for those simple, spent, modern-day moccasins I had ransomed at Quincy Market. Instead I had to go barefoot or sport that pair of garish blemishes. They were the footwear of abomination, the badge of my repatriation from road rat to spoiled brat, and my awkwardness in them never abated.

All the balls I had been given for my birthday—which my delicately-trained hands were way too clumsy to throw, much less catch—lay around the ground floor like mines, ready to upset my imbalance in the vicinity of fragile furnishings. A submerged fleet of lazy Susans kept containers in a state of perpetual rotation, leaving me clumsily capsizing the little vessels, sending contents careening. Entropy reigned, and wherever I walked I was its unwitting envoy, always knocking things over, setting unexpected pinwheels spinning, tripping booby traps. On city streets, I had never had any difficulty avoiding swerving bikes or speeding motorists. Here in utopia, however, the meagerest odds and ends were always bobbing and weaving at unfamiliar tempos. Every atom vibrated to a confounding rhythm.

In bed each night, I tossed and turned in the insufferable fluff for hours of sleepless rumination, pining for the cozy reassurance of brick and steel encroaching from all sides and above, the simple satisfactions of a good day's work on the streets of the Beast, the joys of a smooth pick and a clean snatch. I had given it all up, and for what? The mayor's mansion had its amenities, but it was no place like home. After sunset in Ho-Ho-Kus, senses were inundated by the residue of smug suburban serenity: warm-lighted windows one by one yielding to TV's blue-hued idylls, the baleful barking of neighborhood dogs who had slept all day and eaten kingly suppers, and, seasoning everything, a viridian proliferation of vegetation, sickeningly saturated with smelly chlorophyll, respiring the foul flavor of photosynthesis into the crypt-like cool of evening. At dawn, the din of crickets gave way to mornings fraught with blinding sunlight and the cycle started all over again. Who could stand it? Day in and out, the dreadful grind of what year-round slackers cynically call "summer vacation" droned on in dreary indistinction.

Since the moment I had heard of my parents' earnest to resume guardianship, I had gradually discovered the crux of what had always been my simple wish: I wanted a map to a couple of untidy stones I could spruce up, shed token tears over, and then be finished with; to have a clue as to whether I was Catholic, Jewish, Protestant, Muslim, or other, descendant of Curwen, Irving, or Prynn. I wanted to imagine life with a last name. I would have privately preserved the patronymic and publicly remained Fast Eddie so as not to malign the echo of my ancestry. To have known merely that I had a surname, were it Mann or Munster: Certainly such meager irrigation would have more than satisfied the thirst at the source of my being, but instead I had been drowned in a deluge of unwanted knowledge. It was all too much, what I had ended up inheriting. A naïve presumption which had sent me to seek out simple genealogy had instead landed me an indenture of domesticity. So single-mindedly had I pursued the abstraction of discovering my heritage that I had never allowed for the possibility of corporeal custody. I asked for it. I wished that instead I had just turned myself in on the stoop at Faneuil Hall or been nabbed by that sneaker freak Mano. I knew better than ever the accuracy of that aphorism about what you wish for, and what you get when the gods want to punish you.

It might have helped my spirits to try pickpocketing for old times' sake, but my pilot light had been extinguished. The will to pick had been lost with the old shoes. Now that I myself had a wallet, I was too full of dread and guilt to contemplate even recreational thievery. I had become one of them. Every day I went out and placed myself in danger's way, but no matter how much I tried to get someone to pick, stick, 'nap, or otherwise nab me, I always walked the streets of Pauly's town unmolested. I let the leather lip poke out of my pants on the bus and pretended to fall asleep, but no fellow came along to tug. Not even by rattling a sock full of fifty-dollar coins in the most anemic light of pre-dawn, back-alley, mid-summer suburbia could I summon a charitable soul to unburden me. I couldn't pay someone to rob me.

Early on, I had tried misplacing the wallet, dropping it in a dumpster, knowing even as I did so what a pathetic maneuver it was.

"Mom?"

"In here, honey," she called from the study. She was on the exercise machine, a tantalizing sight: Merry, in low-neck leotard, scaling the side of a mountain that wasn't even there. She pushed a lever and the entire contraption dipped her into some all-fours variation, a cross between stalking cat and knocked-up cow. I tried to look away, but my discomfort was just redoubled when I realized she had set up two full-length mirrors: one a few feet in front of the machine, the other right behind. I had strayed in a pumpkin patch of reduplicating boobs, reiterative tits. Lost in her funhouse, I could see my mouth hanging open in the infinite reflections. There was no closing.

Breathless, forced to focus on her esoteric ascent, I was trying to explain: "Pickpocketed . . . busy street . . . can't be sure how it happened . . ." when the phone rang. It was the chief of police calling to say a billfold had been retrieved and my operator's license was inside. Did I want to come pick it up or would I prefer to have it delivered?

"How about losing those glasses while you're at it?" Merry teased. "Pauly will pay for the laser correction. Fifteen minutes and you're twice as handsome."

When we went to pick it up at city hall, the cool, new ten-G note was still there. Pauly's supercilious smirk made me paranoid he was deliberately doing all this to drive me crazy.

The Ho-Ho-Kus sanitation worker who had found it received a decoration for faithful service.

Audiences with a few local toughs made it clear to me that, although Pauly was mayor, Ho-Ho-Kus and most of the region around was not-so-secretly controlled by that crime boss of old, familiar alias: Apple Jack. Nothing went down without his say-so. Apple Jack ran operations large and small out of a dusty old virtual reality parlor in Paramus, on the other side of the river and the wrong side of the tracks, but the badass boss was rarely seen in the dim, blinking light of Adelle's Penny Arcade.

He had named it after his old flame. At the entrance, a faded poster memorialized the fabled figure, a fortune teller of ancient fame with auburn hair, drawn face, and hollow eyes who, while blind to the material world, could reputedly perceive the future with flawless acuity. Her unearthly visage loomed over the image of an opaque ball composed—as suggested by the illustrated glint—of exquisite crystal. "MADAME ADELLE," read deco lettering, "ASTOUNDING ORACLE." Adelle's "pennies" were credits on plastic cards with imbedded debit chips. Her silhouette was embossed on one side; printed on the other, the dictum: DEUS EX MACHINA.

Apple Jack's Paramus outfit was built on an army of imps a little like road rats. His penny pickers—juvenile cybernauts hooked on VR—ran numbers, perpetrated break-ins, and vandalized the property of delinquent debtors in exchange for the occasional crust of bread and a few arcade credits. In an ingenious piece of personnel management, Apple Jack paid kids with the dummy debit cards he manufactured himself for use in Adelle's Arcade. Even hustlers, bookies, and smugglers gave him shit for so shafting his supplicants, though they were just jealous of how effectively he exacted tribute while in return providing only a fickle flight of fancy for the strung-out cyberaddicts. Already made of gold, Apple Jack didn't stand to profit much from anybody's demise. The freaky despot got involved in others' affairs just for the sake of fucking things up. The principle of asserting his dominance, meanwhile messing with the many lives of the little people, was pretense enough. However much commoners complained, nobody, not even the mayors and cops, ever challenged him. Pauly, having pulled himself up by those fabled bootstraps, identified with his electorate by promoting old-fashioned values and made Merry keep down with the Joneses by doing her own house cleaning, but he, together with thousands of other rats and masters, was just another one of Apple Jack's marionettes.

The first time I went to Adelle's Arcade I became fascinated by the eerie part of the parlor specializing in antique games, from turn-of-the-millennium first-person-shooter all the way back to pinball. This would be a good place to keep my fingers limber, I considered, in case I ever chanced to return to the old trade. Rumor had it that Adelle, all washed up, lived in a back room between burnt motherboards and plywood casings, boxed in by the obsessed Apple Jack, who kept her hidden from life and light. The door was supposedly left unlocked, although in fact one could not be sure, nobody ever having been observed going in or coming out. A hand-lettered sign was posted there, a dreadful dare to the fool who might entertain the idea of passage: THIS MEANS YOU, MOTHERFUCKER. It did not say do not enter. It didn't have to. Nobody even risked walking close enough to accidentally brush up against the door. This was the beauty of Apple Jack's eloquent authority. It never occurred to anyone to toy with the idea of what might happen. We exchanged our twenties for Adelle's pennies and went from game to game, content to traverse virtual wildernesses and battle imaginary evils rather than mess with anything so hopelessly unknown as Apple Jack's back room. After all, only onscreen did a man have multiple lives.

I don't know where the money went, but I managed, at first frugally, then recklessly, to spend it. Ten thousand was more than had been dropped on my account in the fifteen years preceding. Granted, a soda in the suburbs cost fifty bucks and a slice of pizza a hundred, but I was not used to stopping for these indulgences between two such superfluous activities as, say, sleep and arcade. Dropping off, I always left the contents of my pocket there on the bedside table. One morning, after I had managed to nearly empty the wallet, I awoke and discovered it contained a fresh note. All the worthlessness I had reclaimed was ruined by one stroke of Pauly's reckless generosity. Every week or so, when the load became light and I had nearly succeeded in squandering the unsolicited gains, the funds were deviously replenished. This happened again and again. I lost track of how many grand.

The bed, the sneaks, the sunlight, and the wallet were bad enough, but in a short time I became aware of the most awkward reconditioning factor by far: the underthings. On the day I had arrived, the chest had been stocked with two plastic-wrapped ten-packs. Since the day Merry had insisted that I deposit dirty underwear there, in the bin by the bathroom door, the prospect of her defiling her nostrils by lifting out a florid passel of socks and briefs had sent me into paroxysms of self-revulsion. I had not counted on this obvious process when acceding to the drawers full of white stuff. From the information on the labels, I perceived that the items were manufactured nearby. Maybe Pauly had political ties on the inside—he got them for me for free, I reasoned, and they were disposable, the bin emptied straight into the Ho-Ho-Kus incinerator. I changed daily in an effort to use up the neatly creased pieces in my drawers and call their bluff. I believed that if I hurried through these, new packages would appear. Instead, the same pairs started coming around clean. This underwear scenario had all other humiliations beat. It made me want to die before emitting another by-product. It was nobody's business but my own to handle my skivvies. However frequently I managed to start fresh, I could not ponder objectively the imprint of shame on each article. As a rat, I had spent too many years wearing the same pants for too many weeks ever to wash the stain from subconscious. Like the homicidal lady who can't shout out the phantom spot, I saw skid marks every day I stripped to the bare essentials. Although I never chanced to observe Merry emptying the hamper, imagination reeled at the prospect of her bent over the washer, mouth turned down in disgust to find, dried on the fly, little dandelion patches of my pee. How harrowing the prospect of the innocent woman handling the perennially mud-tracked fabric that got pinched at my perineum!

Want to mess with a boy's head while he's hitting the peak of puberty? Move him in with a mother-stranger who's got a proclivity for exhibitionism. Merry had a habit of leaving her hand-washed bras drying on the downstairs bathroom shower curtain rod. Whenever I was on the can my glance grazed that way. I was stricken by ruminations on the bloom of her breasts. Had I suckled those mammaries? If so, I had no memory, and this poverty enraged me, fanning an anguish that in turn stoked the coals of my longing. I daydreamed for hours about what it might have been like. Brain boiled with humiliating names: Percy, Fauntleroy, mollycoddle, mama's boy. There were a million terms, medical and menial, for my condition. Thoughts about Merry consumed what insular serenity was left. Somewhere back there, the big sneakers had introduced the irrational inkling that, much in the same way I sullied rugs, I might be at risk of upsetting Merry's chastity. Gods, help me! What was it, newly blossoming in subconscious, that caused me to obsess so over her chest? Mother who birthed me, betwixt whose legs I had burgeoned! Mother who had presumably, at least until her paternal intervention, nursed me! Mother!

Merry continued to peek in on my reading, sleeping, brushing, washing, and kept on suffocating me with breakfast-table embraces. Over and above the already-arduous job of surviving sixteen, it seemed especially dangerous getting to know a mother this late in the game. When a baby is a baby, then babying is innocent, but since I had skipped all the do-do doing and weenie washing, dormant solicitude had metamorphosed into something sick and sinister. Now I could not bask innocently in all the stifling affection. Testosterone had taken care of that. Latency had turned natal innocence into a very adultish lust. No doubt Merry's attentions were well intentioned, but the sickeningly sweet odor of my perverse reactions permeated the air and summoned legions of black flies. I was rotten, corrupted. All day I dreamed about sex.

Merry's fawning just aggravated my antagonism for Pauly, whose pretense of obliviousness in the face of the maternal indiscretions made him an indifferent accomplice, a latent fetishist, or—worst of all—a blind ignoramus. "Dad" became a tough concept to wrap my head around. It had to do with all the little, nit-picky things that I should have worked through harmlessly as a toddler and juvenile and probably gotten over with by the time I was a teen. According to all the books, I would have become jealous, bitten his finger, hit him, cried, rebelled, et cetera, all in the first eighteen months. But now, after years of sublimated patriphobia, the all-too-real old sot really started to bug me. The delight with which he simpered, "Cool shoes, huh?" engendered in me what I imagine to be the most toxic of filial attitudes: arrogance. How could Merry stand the man? The thought of our underpants commingling in her washer hurtled me into private fits of sanguinary hostility.

Dejection kept sending me across the bridge into Paramus, where I spent most of my days vegetating at Adelle's Penny Arcade. I became a burnout, an adolescent with a vengeance, sublimating my murderous tendencies into slumping, smoking, sulking, and (by the dexterity I had developed in my former trade) excelling at manipulation of all the buttons, track balls, flippers, joysticks, pistol grips, and power gloves Adelle's had to offer. Whenever I snuffed a man on screen, I pretended it was Pauly.

With a wallet always full of money to blow on pennies and a lot of time to kill, I fell in with a brat who, if not my kind, was at least kindred, a penny picker who hustled petty gamblers on corners claim-staked by the boss. His name was Sumner, but the rest of the penny pickers called him Some Nerd. He slept inside a cardboard box that by day served as a bent-out-of-shape three-card-monte table on Paramus sidewalks. At Adelle's, I often played doubles and sort of became chums with him. Some Nerd's reflexes sucked, so usually he would stand around and get fed up waiting for me to finish with my umpteenth extra life.

"Time to die, four-eyes."

"Shut up, Some Nerd. I need some simulated slaughter. My parents are getting on my nerves."

"Don't sweat it, Eddie. So your folks are jerks. You're lucky you ended up in Jersey. There's a tradition here of saying things like 'parents suck' and meaning it."

Instead of just playing MP, the juke box at Adelle's was loaded with old-fashioned compact discs featuring an ancient mode known as rock 'n' roll. On one popular selection, a gentleman named Jim, long-since disappeared, crooned a spooky poem about obsolescence.

I asked Some Nerd whether this was what people used to call hip-hop.

"Hell no. Heavy metal, which came much later."

In an eerie spoken section, the singer, one of the weirdest werewolves to self-destruct under the influence of all the odd drugs they had back in his day, performed a little schizophrenic oratory. "Father?" "Yes, son." "I want to kill you . . . Mother? I want to—" The accompaniment crescendoed and what he said in the end was unintelligible, but I sure sympathized with the sound.

Walking back from the arcade across the Saddle River bridge, I saw a promising sign. Pauly had urged me, as the mayor's son, to do some kind of public service. ("Nothing too arduous, preferably not blue collar.") At first I had moodily refused to respond, muttering under my breath where he could put his public service, but a billboard gave me an idea of one place I might enjoy clocking some hours. I volunteered to be a crisis counselor on a suicide hotline.

The coordinator explained that the job hinged upon an ability to distinguish cranks and crackpots from at-risk self-immolators. A common question to slip in early might be: "Have you thought about killing yourself today?" followed by "Have you thought about how you would do it?" We had to be able to triage whether each call was a) a lonely liar tying up the line, b) a depressive sort who should be urged to pursue treatment, or c) a real candidate for the bridges where the phone number was found. On the training exam, one section tested the counselor's discrimination on the basis of the caller's opening line. EXAMPLE: *"All my plants are dying?"* CIRCLE ONE: High Risk, Possible Risk, No Risk. Born blessed with a nose for nuance, I was the only one in the volunteer pool who identified correctly: Get dibs on the music collection, friends, 'cause this one is going to *jump*.

Fielding calls was a crash course in pop psychology, and I defied the guidebook by psychoanalyzing. I could swap self-destructive scenarios with the introverts, trade bluffs with the exhibitionists, conjure laughter in the depressed, cheerfully convince the psychotics they were just being paranoid, and hedge bets with the real paranoids to make them believe they were merely neurotic. Although I cannot be sure about the long-term effectiveness of my strategies, I suspect that, if nothing else, I did some of the callers good by demonstrating a personality that was, even more than their own, cracked, crumbling, and rapidly washing away. I did not tell them about my own insane parental situation, although many of the callers were teenagers living at home who "hated them," "wished they were dead," "couldn't take it any more," and in a few cases had already become embroiled in dark and dangerous relations with one adult or the other. Instead, I accomplished my pathological passion play by instant and uncanny identification with the mechanisms of the caller's morose ruminations. I knew all about toxic thought, and accurately described the nuances of different sorts of psychic sizzle that accompany each aberrant mind cycle.

I learned that, among teenagers, potential for trouble has a lot to do with creativity. Newly possessing all the overpowering insight and energy of adulthood, a teen can in his restlessness either become skeptical of all the institutions (educational, legal, parental) that have up until that time been taken for tacit authorities, or else attempt an idealistic embrace of adult society and its conventions. Either way, the shift involves terrific risks, because despite his enlightenment, imagination, and will to respond to everything he sees, the adolescent is not yet equipped with the emotional means. It is one of the arduous asynchronicities of youth, a retarded ability to harness creativity in spite of extraordinary energy. The worst-case upshot: Constructive potential sours, turns rancid, and becomes the curds of destruction. Every vandal is a Van Gogh, each thief Marcel Marceau. Even in the most violent gang you have the potential for an ingenious klezmer band. Suicides are almost always promising poets.

I came up against every kind of pathology in the book.

More often than not, the dominant complex also concealed its complementary opposite: inferiority/superiority, persecution/castration, Electra/Diana. There were not a few callers who in the first minute I could tell had imbibed a jigger of recombinant disorders. As for existential cynicism, I was king. People accidentally presume that the dilemma of being involves implicit persistence and requires extraordinary justification—even under great adversity—to settle on stopping, whereas in reality we enjoy a rare and privileged prerogative, that light switch dangling in front of our noses, to die at any moment. The real absurdity, a by-product of almost bovine conformity, is when an individual confronting the question of whether to live one more day presumes the choice prescribed. The matter is not *why go on?* but *why not die?* I could speak convincingly about that place where a person was ready to shoot, swallow, slice, jump, what have you. Not only had I been there, the more I thought about it, the more I seemed to toe that edge every day.

The line was always understaffed after midnight, so I pulled a lot of lobster shifts. Within a few weeks, I had developed a little cadre of malcontents who asked for me by name, spreading the word among their morbid friends to call in and try this kid on for size. Certainly, my methods were unorthodox. It was not an advice line. It was not even characterized as crisis counseling, merely intervention. The rest we were supposed to hand off to the pros. I doubt I would have lasted a day on the lines had the supervisor not been narcoleptic.

Merry and Pauly, self-confessed pantheists who for the sake of the electorate attended ecumenical services, urged me to choose a religion. Irreligion was also an option. They were surprised when I selected Hindu, and wondered aloud whether I might not prefer an order with more ascribants in Ho-Ho-Kus, maybe even a congregation. I didn't budge, so they bought me comic books on Brahma. It wasn't this incarnation, creator, who interested me. I preferred Siva and Vishnu's aspects of the triad, especially when the latter, by his title Jagannath, came crushing in his trademark car, radiant and unyielding, steadfast in the doctrine of destruction. Wasn't subtraction of the subject the surest, shortest path to obliterating all? My ideal heroine was the suttee, the widow who devotedly ascends her husband's pyre.

Somewhere in here I stopped wearing underwear.

Every day I went home with a more bolstered bad attitude. Although at first I tried to suppress it, I could not hide my malcontentment. I was alternately overtaken by brooding spells and fits of mania. I adopted the game junkie convention of communicating only in grunts.

Merry's diagnosis, shouted from inside the folks' shower: "What Eddie needs is a girlfriend."

"He'll be happier once school starts and he makes a couple of friends," Pauly called back, probably from the can. His patronizing tone brewed my mounting mistrust, a malignancy which, bottled up as it was, fermented into fetid contention. If only Merry and Pauly had known what black ruminations I was entertaining about what I really needed, and how each of them were intimately involved!

I was glad when classes began, if for nothing else than another excuse to get out of the house, where I was always on the verge of causing grievous harm to contents or occupants. I enjoyed some modicum of success in physical education, managing to distinguish myself not through team sports but with gymnastics. All of those stunts that Olympians make look so easy on TV? They really were easy for me. The beam was putty beneath my broad base, and I accomplished inversions almost unconsciously. The parallel bars were a stroll around the block: I flung myself on them, did a couple of bent revolutions, and with a flourish got spat out the other end. High jumps, long jumps, and pole vaults found me nonchalantly launching myself into low atmospheric orbit, breaking all the dusty town records. Amidst classmates' snickering at my you-know-whats, the only way I knew I had done something exceptional was by the dumbfounded expression of the patronizing instructor, who wore a bronze medal over his muscle–T for winning third place in some or another long-ago event.

To my parents' dismay I found no allies at school. There was nobody for me to identify with in the scout troops, homecoming committees, and skate gangs of suburban Jersey. Even if there had been other delinquents enrolled at Ho-Ho-Kus High, road rats by nature don't make friends. We do not get in one another's way. We certainly don't mess with each other's undershorts. The only recourse for maintenance of my sanity was to bury myself in books and turn the black musings inward. I devoured the literature of elective death. For show-and-tell in social studies, I came dressed as a Samurai and simulated seppuku, the ancient Japanese art of auto-disem-bowelment. The gym teacher tried to get me to join the track team, but I was already too immersed in the after-school cynicism of arcade players.

That first marking period I thought I might have been in

line for at least one A, but then misfortune struck my peaceable little oasis of the gymnasium. It was a mild day on which the morning sun, shining through arched windows, was split into beams by criss-crossing girders and illuminated long shafts of floating motes. I was sitting on the polished floor, daydreaming, waiting for class to begin, when a warm finger caressed my face and thoughts migrated to Merry. An innocent little reverie: I come home from school, the autumn breeze blowing, and she has baked something good to eat. I sit at the kitchen table, where all is bird song and sunlight and it is somehow not irritating. She bends over me with a steaming slice of banana bread and accidentally, through parting folds of blouse, I catch a glimpse of her bulging, unfettered breasts.

I shook myself out of the idle, but in my baggy yellow sweat pants a sleeping troll had stirred. The teacher was talking to me.

"What?"

"I said it's your turn, Corrente." About once a month, each of us was required to lead exercises, the little battery of calisthenics that opened every class. It was a piece of cake: a few windmills, some toe-touches, and ten squat-thrust jumping jacks. This phys ed teacher, a fanatic for warm-up regimentation, capped his crusade by going through the roster in alphabetical order and insisting that every student take a turn as leader. Refusal resulted in an automatic F for the quarter, so even those slackers with reputations for the most uncooperative behavior invariably obeyed. I had already pantomimed my way through two such displays and with the jump of each jack been painfully conscious of the chuckled response to my superior sneakers and their resounding *smack!*

Under the current circumstances, however, submission would leave me deeply exposed.

"There must be a mistake," I said, bending forward and folding my arms across my lap to conceal the convulsing creature. Hadn't we just finished the alphabet the day before?

"A couple of kids missing today. Both Athanaeleas and Bacchi are absent."

It was beginning to make awful sense. Never had anyone been so brash as to simply refuse the task and defiantly down a round, resounding zero for the course. Still, however short and simple the humiliation of reluctantly taking a moment in the spotlight, performing a few lackluster stretches, mumbling and-a-one-and-a-twos while the teacher robustly bellowed *I can't hear you!* from the back of the gymnasium, leading exercises was still considered a sufficiently sissy-like surrender. A few bullies with reputations to protect calculated ahead, kept track of their assigned day, and made a point of not showing up. The instructor had a habit of simply skipping to the next name, allowing the absentee to thereby absorb the lesser penalty of a no-show.

"It says right here," the gym teacher, finger in the infallible attendance book, said with finality, "Corrente. Come on. Up and at 'em."

I cursed my irksome, newfound name. What good had it done me over the years I hadn't known it? And now look at the ill it caused! All eyes on me, sitting Indian-style, barely concealing the poker in my pants, there was no way that I, wearing loose sweats and sans underwear, could stand in this state, the admiral at attention.

"Teach, I'll take the F."

When the report card came I wanted Pauly to get angry at me. I was prepared to be scolded—wished for it, even. Maybe a little friction would diffuse the familial ambivalence gradually mounting into fury. Of course you could call it hypocrisy. While conspicuously skipping classes and between shifts at suicide intervention, all I did was distract myself with virtual escapes at Adelle's. I did not care about suburban school, which, although spread out over five days, was almost as good as Shep's brand of concentrated education, and yet I wanted my old man to take responsibility for my indifference. After all, hadn't fathers been put here in order to address precisely these kinds of discrepancies? I needed to be chastised, castigated, grounded, damn it! Shep would have made me stay back with the snot-nosed brats and repeat the section until I learned my lesson.

"Grades don't matter, son," Pauly said instead. "You'll graduate. The important thing is PR. Just stay out of trouble: no hookers, no cybertropics, or at least"—he winked conspiratorily—"don't get caught."

Pauly thought he was being cool, but I saw through the illusion to his lame, depraved manipulation of all the teachers, truant officers, and crossing guards of Ho-Ho-Kus. Who was he trying to kid? Pauly was just another pawn in Apple Jack's game. Although the entire town might be a stage for his petty megalomania, Pauly was no more his own man than the pack masters back in the Beast.

That night I was playing doubles with Some Nerd, whipping the pants off him in a good old bout of Joust, a vintage game with pole-fighting knights mounted on flying ostriches.

"Come on, Eddie, hurry up and die already."

"You'd still be playing, Some Nerd, if your mother hadn't huffed so much paint thinner when you were in utero."

"Oh yeah?" His own head full of inhalants, the twitchy kid delivered the insult that planted the demon seed: "Your old lady's a ho."

"What'd you say?"

"You can't see straight even with those goofy goggles, Eddie. The mayor's not even your dad."

I lost my man, pushed that punk to the ground, and fled the arcade, running back across the bridge to Ho-Ho-Kus instead of waiting around to get my ass kicked by a posse of penny pickers.

Worse than Some Nerd's aspersion was the emotion it conjured within. The net effect advanced a premise I had secretly hypothesized after getting dragged down to Jersey, only never articulated. I wished my detractor was right. It was the inverse of that longing that had pissed me off after Shep's insult: this time, that I might actually be oblivious to the answer of my parentage. After all, Pauly really irritated me; and Merry: How else could I ever justify having the hots for her? All those years wishing and yet now preferring to be right back where I had begun, a bastard—that was the most disturbing prospect of all.

When I got home, Merry was crouched on the couch and the blue light of the TV shone through her sheer gown, showing me a skin-deep X-ray. Patiently painting her toenails red, she didn't look up. The doyens of doubt—her petite feet—were out in the open. I couldn't kick the sticky conviction that they were materially too flimsy to belong to anybody who could have made me. Genetically, some mortar is incontrovertibly maternal—hair fiber, for instance. Science has shown that a boy takes after his mother from head to toe, even if everything in between ("He's got your eyes/ankles/nose/knees/mouth/ *wow!*") flows from the father. I steeled my resolve and repeated what Some Nerd had said. Rather, I paraphrased, revising in the interest of euphemism. "Mom, someone at the arcade mentioned something today. I was wondering: Do you think maybe you and Dad might have adopted the wrong kid?"

"Oh! E!" Merry said, exhaling heavily. In the midst of my stupor of adolescent brooding, I could not be sure when she had started to use this sobriquet, but it was better than the cryptic *edh*. "It's just another street urchin jealous of your good fortune. Bring me the cotton balls, will you?"

"I'm sorry, Mom . . ." I picked up the box of fluff from the coffee table. Merry was bent well over her leg so I had to approach close. ". . . It's just that—*muf!*" Despite having her hands full, Merry managed to lock me in a bosomy embrace, pushing my head into her chest to shut me up. "Boys get jealous when a mother and son are as close as you and me, honey."

I broke away. "*Puh!*—okay, whatever you say."

Taking off my sneakers in the mud room, I noticed something funny. The star was beginning to peel off one of the tongues. However underwhelmed I had been by this pair, I was not used to poor stitching from my cobbler of choice. Upon closer examination, it became evident that someone had tampered with the uppers. There was an alien emblem underneath the star. These weren't Cons at all, but a reviled brand: Adidas, by Zeus!

"Oh, sure," Merry confirmed. "Daddy didn't like any of the

Converse kind. But he knew how attached you were to the idea so he had the salesman switch the logo."

A rage rose up in me nothing short of patricidal. The wallet of no escape, the give-or-take grades, and the spirit-sapping shoes—all of these configured themselves into a constellation of manipulation that Pauly was perpetrating on my person. His perversion for taking over a son's autonomy had been overstimulated from such long dormancy. Now it was not enough that I had adopted his stupid surname. Pauly wanted to depersonalize me completely, to brainwash the individual Eddie and end up with a puppet to do his blowhard bidding and parrot his pathetic legacy.

I grumbled, "I'm going to bed."

"By the way," Merry said, "Daddy's gone to a convention in Atlantic City—it's just you and me tonight. Sweet dreams, honey."

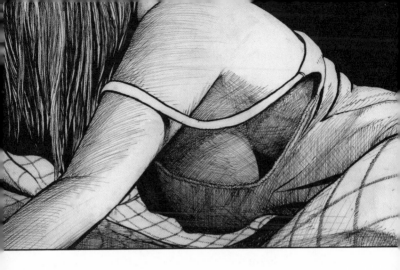

I was covered in honey. Or I was honey. This was not offensive to me, not even disagreeable. It was not sticky, or the stickiness was not evident. It was a warm, comfortable medium that made everything formless and delicately kinetic. I moved languorously through a labyrinthine network composed of white walls at gently beveled angles. The feeling was not claustrophobic. I was liquid. My whole golden body flowed. I held an amorphous, dripping hand to my face. It shined with light as if from inside.

A figure approached. It was my mother, or a mother—she did not resemble Merry-as-in-Christmas Corrente. All the same, I recognized her as a mother force, a potent, pungent assailant of affection, an extortionist of epileptic emotion. I was glad to see her, or anyway I was free from ambivalence about my fondness for her, for anyone, for whatever companion I might encounter in this queer environment, alternating now between maze and a vast, desolate plane. After all, I was honey. There was nothing that my mind or my body could do in transgression of any exterior code. She was moving with just as much fluidity as me, although she was of flesh and blood and wearing clothes: pants and a V-neck T-shirt, the collar plunging precipitously past the cleft in her swelling bosom. She reached her arms out and we seemed to be heading towards a slow-motion embrace. Doting devotion had molded her idyllic face into a simpering expression, with an idiot grin reciprocally palpable in my own ambrosial jaw.

She was almost upon me when a change took place. While she maintained a motherly form, her pace faltered and molecular make-up metamorphosed. She became a dense and quivering body of bees. It was beautiful, this apiarian ballet in shapely, maternal form—lovely enough so that for a moment I forgot who I was. But I was honey, and my oblivion evaporated in an instant when that buzzing air force broke ranks and swarmed, ravishing my mellifluent essence. Everything shifted into the frenzied speed of a fast feed. Mother was nowhere to be seen. The insatiable beasts were all over me. They ate my eyes that I could no more see, then no longer did I have me to be. I was not sure whether I was being transformed into or altogether replaced, atom for atom, by wax. I went from fluid to rigid. The bees had at once consumed my substance and entombed my absence in a corporeal comb. Their cocoon left what context might have been me, material or no, immobilized.

The high-pitched, howling drone of the voracious bees' ravenous feast reverberating away in the dark, desolate bedroom, I awoke all wet, trying to thrash but merely spasming, genuinely immobilized by a tangle of soggy sheets binding my limbs. The cotton clung to my body like the coating on a cough drop. I had squirmed and wrestled for merely a moment when a blinding light burst in from the hall and I gazed up helplessly to see Merry in the doorway. I was mute, but the interval I spent in deliberating what to say was a fatal one. She jumped into my bed and threw her arms around my shoulders. Startled, not yet fully in this dimension, I cowered and let out a shriek.

"It's okay, Eddie. It was just a bad dream."

Not yet in control, I whimpered, "How do you know?"

"I was having trouble sleeping when I heard the cutest little squeaking noise." She turned my head and pushed my nose into her perfumed chest. "It was so sweet! You sounded just like a puppy!"

My face pressed into the loose collar of her nightgown, I was still paralyzed, regaining my senses, when I recognized with some trepidation that those senses were now utterly flooded by her stimuli: frilly convolutions, fragrant hair, rapid breath, heaving bosom.

"I'm all right," I said. "Please go back to bed." I tasted the salt of a sweat not my own.

"But I can't sleep. And you, poor baby, your bed is soaked. Come lie in Daddy's place."

Stiffening, I said, "I'll be fine."

"Don't you want to tell Mommy about your dream?"

"No!" I said with a start. My desperate tone made her tighten the iron clasp around my neck. I became rigid. Over the course of childhood I had escaped from straitjacket, lobster trap, and handcuffs, but I had no idea how I was going to wrest my way out of this one. "I wasn't having a nightmare," I began, not knowing where I was going with this.

She wasn't listening. "Jeez, if the sheets are this sticky, your pajamas must be sopping wet, too. How did you get so tangled?"

"As a matter of fact, I wasn't even asleep."

She wasn't taking any. "Come on, get yourself out of those clothes."

"Ma!" I cried. She waited, gazing lovingly down at me with all the patience of a cage. An exterior intelligence, speaking with my voice, seemed to have overtaken me. "The truth is," I lied, "you're interrupting a very important Hindu ceremony. The sheets—they're wet for the ritual."

"What? Oh! my baby! I'm sorry," Merry said, loosening a little. "What's the . . . what's the ritual for?" she said with a thrill.

"Virility," I spouted.

"Gosh, Eddie. I'm impressed." The chains melted away. Merry was retreating in the dim room, backpedaling out into the bright hall. Light silhouetted her curves through the gossamer nightie. Before gently pulling the door closed, she whispered, "Listen, if your little ritual is successful and you can't get to sleep, come down the hall and let Mommy take care of you, 'kay?"

I listened for her footsteps to go quiet at the end of the hall and began mutely working my way free from the cocoon of wet sheets, a task that took almost ten minutes of strenuous exertion. Exhausted, I tiptoed into the bathroom, locked the door, stripped off the wet bedclothes and toweled myself dry. I did not dare shower. I wouldn't have been surprised if Merry had returned and offered to scrub my back. I put on jeans, a sweatshirt, and the shoes of deceit. I need to get out of here, I thought, and shut off these sinister thoughts. I knew what I had to do in lieu. I picked up the wallet and a handful of change from the bedside table, depositing these burdens in my pockets, then slipped down the stairs, out the back door, and into the street, the buzzing still echoing in my ears.

It took two hours pretending to watch the cybernauts play VR to sidle up to the door. I stood with my back to the sign, taking in the sum effect of the whole room, and for an instant out of time the world seemed intangible. Everyone else was intent, each absorbed in his or her own synthetic environment, a still-life of dumb-struck, brain-dead satisfaction.

THIS MEANS YOU, MOTHERFUCKER.

I just touched the knob, already promising myself, in a futile attempt to calm my wildly beating heart, that I would not actually enter, that I was only curious to make physical contact with the mythic portal. Suddenly everything went pitch dark. Even in my state of extraordinary adrenal alertness, I could not ascertain whether I had blacked out. An untenable stretch of time passed during which I might have sojourned to the curving edge of the expanding universe, but then I realized I had somehow been spirited into the forbidden back room of Adelle's Penny Arcade. In a cruel accession of destiny, a snippet of deliberation had been lost to me. How had I been robbed of the chance to chicken out? What if I had been detected? I pressed an ear to the crack of the doorway and listened for a commotion, but there were just the muffled, mollifying booms and pings of pilgrims absorbed religiously at their rituals. My heart was up in my throat and I was too terrified to back out. I tried to calm myself with deep breaths while my eyes adjusted—given the usual acuity of my night vision, an absurdly long interval. A peculiar, viscous quality to the air left the center of the room saturated with darkness. I focused on the far edge of the ceiling, where an anemic glow seeping in through soot-smudged window panes made a grimy garland along the top of the wall. Finally, I saw her. She was crouched right in front of me, the spookiest old gypsy staring with glazed eyes from behind plate glass. I froze. At her belt, a little ledge was covered with cards only slightly less dingy than the tablecloth of rotting felt. They were face down, and nothing about the backs advertised the likelihood of anything being printed on the fronts. After ten seconds of ear-thumping paralysis I thought to wonder about Adelle's unblinking lids. She seemed hypnotized. However terrified, I had to try to get a closer look. For better stealth, I took off the clunky Adidases and left them by the door.

Adelle turned out to be a mechanized mannequin, a metallic mermaid whose torso, instead of turning fishy, was fused into a blocky box at the base of her transparent tank. There was a coin slot where her navel might have been, maybe a little lower. Static stars and flaccid ribbons had been pasted patternlessly around the inside of the booth. I strained to read the writing, ornate faux hieroglyphs that time had partly rubbed away from the casing: YOUR FORTUNE A PENNY.

There was no swiper for my penny card, and Adelle's slot rejected all the usual denominations: I tried ten-, twenty-, and fifty-dollar coins. None of them fit the sliding steel slot that presumably would catapult the proper piece inside. Adelle would have been a bitch to trip: A diminutive eyelet would not admit any of the common slugs, the mechanism prohibited insertion of a skeleton key, and her case—of an antique cast that, for its heft, could have been iron—was impossible to crack. Even if I had managed to figure out the trick, I doubted whether she would still operate. I had decided it was not too late to try finding a window or vent through which to escape and vow to never look back on, much less speak of, this dangerous game, when I was struck by a strange feeling, a jiggle in my pants like a Mexican jumping bean. I fished in the denim pocket and what did I pull out but One Cent. Funny, I had never thought of it as money, this chump's charm. *Are you lucky?*

I tried the coin in the notch—it fit!—thrust the protuberance into the heart of the machine, and held it there for a second. Heart skipped a beat as the bodkin stuck. The trough burst back out—empty! A second second: Nothing happened. Adelle seemed not to like it. My brass had been too brash, unpalatable to the venerable seer. I had plunged in a poisonous plug and jammed her contraption, at once executing antique medium and forsaking trusty One Cent. A cosmic sense of loss came pouring in through a coin-sized quark in my chest. I was ready to crawl into a corner and curl up with the rest of the dilapidated has-beens when I heard a faint whirring coming from far away. Then all the world crashed into being.

Adelle accepted my suppository, swallowed, and sprang to life. Hands of crumbling plaster stiffly lifted little cards, unjointed arms crossed and recrossed her airtight atmosphere in hypnotic gymnastics impossible not merely for the human form, but, it would seem, for matter at all. Pinwheels spun and streamers streaked about the dusty interior of Adelle's transparent chamber, causing dust bunnies inside the vestibule to awaken from hibernation and explode with ghostly smokes. I agonized to make sense of Adelle's alabaster expression, which remained unchanged. The whole cabinet creaked and croaked with the winding down of robotic clockwork, and Adelle herself—as if animated by some other, unseen, unearthly engine—whined and groaned. What are you trying to say? *Creep? Kraut? Rhine? Rome?* The mummy shuffle sufficiently entranced me so that by the time Adelle's revolutions were done and the room fell abruptly silent, more silent, for the ebbing of the cacophony, than before, it took a second to register that the works below had spit something out. I scooped the cardboard fortune from the repository at Adelle's abstract lap. What was that cold chill emanating from the alcove behind me?

A growl of sour stomach boomed from the resonant darkness. "Curse my goddamn indigestion." Spinning 180, I almost jumped out of my socks. "Boy, you got a fuckin' question?" Before the door loomed a figure somehow darker than shadow, a black hole of form and spirit in whose presence I felt more alone than when it had just been me and the machine. I stole a glance at Adelle. She was silent, stationary, altogether unmoved by my plight. After the intensity of our intimacy, when she had by her wooden gaze penetrated my dilated eyes and fixed on the ineluctable essay of my dormant fortune, she now displayed only mute complicity with the awful drama playing out before her. I felt betrayed, but how could I blame her? After all, the animating impulse was over; the magic had been spent with the penny, One Cent. "Don't make me fart—it'll tear you apart."

In timorous tones, with the upcurled articulation of supplication, I said, "I'm a friend of Apple Jack."

"You smokin' crack? Your answer's wack—a shit full of sack. *I'm* Apple Jack." Out of the abyss emerged the greatest mass of spirit I have ever seen, except that, in the ill-lit back room, it was precisely everything but him I could see. Fluorescent tattoos implied great crushing biceps. A broad rim of lustrous platinum rings delineated flaring nostrils. Green-glowing aquatic goggles reflected fire from no visible source, perhaps the smoldering ignition of my own terror. "I know your daddy," Apple Jack proclaimed, "and he's one dead ducker. You'll get him iced of you don't blow, mother-fucker." A great, flashing swatch of gnashing gold caps briefly illuminated the room while Apple Jack uttered the obscenity: at his feet, my orphaned Adidases. *So long, sneaks.*

Although a warm but not consoling tingle told me that I was quite thoroughly irrigating my britches, I feigned indignation, quarried my last reserves of nerve, and said in tremulous sotto, "What did you call me?"

"You heard me, sucka," Apple Jack huffed. Rolling it over his blood-engorged tongue—which even with twenty feet between us I can attest was cankerous, fetid-smelling, coated with gore, as if for breakfast he had consumed a half-dozen pygmies—he indulgently drew out the insult, lasciviously licking each delectable syllable: "Muh . . . tha . . . fuh . . . ka!" In the four seconds of orthodontic light this gave me, I sprinted between his columnar legs and into the cacophonous parlor. I blasted out Adelle's front door, the full flare of dawn exploding over me, and burned down the street on shoeless feet, Apple Jack ever after casting a terrible golden gleam on my subconscious eye.

I ran through the alleys and abandoned lots of Paramus. I did not know where to go. I only knew I could not go back to Ho-Ho-Kus. Return over the Saddle River would only provoke my own self-destructive strain. Ever since discovering my patrimony, I had entertained escapist ruminations. Now I was a sleepless, guilt-ridden fugitive, and I knew that if I tried crossing the bridge I might not make it to the other side. As with all borderlines, I was of two minds, and I was afraid the spoils might go the way that would have me more intimately familiar with river's bottom. It would do no good to try calling the hotline—I was already hip to that bullshit. Ringing in my ears, Apple Jack's insult, threatening prophetic: *Blow, motherfucker*. On the card Adelle had given me, one line: *PS: He lives.* The combined message was clear: Not-so-naturally did I love my mother, while for my father I would never be anything but trouble. If I didn't make tracks, I risked knocking up the one and off the other. At the outskirts of the city, I squeezed through the steel lips of a Goodwill bin and was swallowed in a tangle of second-hand clothes. I changed my pee-soaked pants and found a pair of mismatched clodhoppers. Lacing up one big wingtip and one worn rubber gunboat, this was all I knew: I wanted the feel of the road, movement more rapid than my defeated feet could bring. I wanted a chariot to spirit me away, out of these towns, and I wanted it fast.

All the options were there on the board at the bus terminal. I fixated on the obvious destination. Should I make my way back to the Beast, resume where I had left off, resign myself to the status of rat, and spend the rest of my days a sideshow sidekick to Shep's petty Svengali? I could almost hear him smugly sensing the return of his prodigal Milquetoast, readying a sharp riposte: "Ha! boy, come back? bad pennies come not sooner."

All the other place names had, during my days operating in and around South Station, provided enchanting distraction for the hapless travelers I sent their ways holding only their tickets. I had imagined them emptying out at the other ends —Fantastic Falls, Big Apple, Boardwalk, et cetera—and patting pockets for a little reassurance, just to discover the disheartening absence. What a way to get to know a place!

Plotting equilaterally on the route map, I located the vertex of Ho-Ho-Kus and the Beast, just above Albany on the Hudson River. As long as I was deliberating, I figured I might as well triangulate. In that accursed wallet there was more than enough money for the fare. I decided to go on a little odyssey.

"Howdy!" the driver, whose badge read "Homer," hailed. Taking my ticket and espying behemoth feet, he added, "Long trip to Troy. With big boats like those you better take the first row."

The suspension was loose and high, the ride like an industrial rock tumbler for the bowels, a centrifuge for the soul. The four-hour trip over awful surfaces turned my insides into ratatouille. In spite of all the discomfort, the bus was a perspective worlds apart from the low, road-hugging lounge chair that had brought me to this part of the world. The limousine had been too terrifying. Every time a truck had passed, I felt certain we were about to get crushed, but here on high I could just let it all go by. In the front seat, I ended up suffering everyone's mass-transit nightmare: being held captive by an endless talker. I could not ask him to please shut up, as he was the operator. In garrulous good humor, Homer narrated the wonders of the road. "I go places. I have adventures. I meet interesting people. Yup, best job there is. You should try it, kid." He added, nodding cockeyed at my huge shoes, "You look like you're cut out for it."

I was lulled by the the bus driver's injunction. Who was to say I had not haplessly happened upon my calling? It made sense, in a way. Why get off the bus at all? By staying, I could make all these piddly towns mere pauses on a perpetual run which would itself become the here-and-now. What better way to live up to my name than to be always on the go? At the time it seemed like fate. In retrospect, I suppose I just gauged, in an unconscious, accelerated way, that it was time to resolve on a regimen that might pilot me through the terrible teens. I required a little self-imposed authority in the absence of an actual role model, something, in short, to keep me and the rest of the Correntes out of trouble.

After he discharged all the passengers, I had Homer make good on his injunction by taking me to an empty parking lot for a little driving lesson. At first press of pedal to the metal, I felt connected with predestiny. My big, ballasted sandbags were just as long as this, the largest of all accelerators. It took me twenty minutes to get the hang of bus-driving. Chalk it up to VR practice at the arcade.

I had my driver's permit, which said I was seventeen, but for a chauffeur's license I'd have to be twenty-one, and I could not use the name Corrente—what if Pauly and Merry tried to track me? So in Troy I ditched the EC ID, inquired at a head shop, got the phone number of a fellow who manufactured fakes, and decided to shut down the teen in me.

"What name do you want on it?"

"Eddie."

"Eddie what?"

"Make it Eddie . . . Swift."

"Hey Frankie!" said the artist to his laminating assistant, "we got a porn star here!"

Aiding my alias back in the early days of my escape was the fact that puberty had hit like a ton of bricks over the summer, filling out my gangly frame, slackening my vocal cords, and sprouting fuzz in all the right places, especially my face. I sported that shadow with all the dolefulness that befits a bandit. It was as if some dark condensation had brought a brown cloud to my countenance, occluding my mouth and effectively eclipsing all distinguishing characteristics.

I marched into the bus-line offices armed with my new

identity and asked for an application. "You sure this is you?" the supervisor said, examining the license.

"Sure I'm sure." He looked down at my big, dissimilar shoes. He must have reasoned that anyone with feet that large had to be older than he looked.

"What days you want?"

"What do you mean?"

"Monday to Friday? Wednesday to Sunday? It has to be a minimum of five, and they have to be consecutive. Company rules."

"Sunday to Saturday would be fine."

"Are you making fun of me, floppy feet?"

"No, sir. I would like to work the whole week. I'm used to it."

"Oh, I see, trying to save up vacation days?"

"I won't take them. Give them to someone else."

"They're non-transferable. And just in case you're thinking of a mad dash to early retirement, they don't roll over at the end of the calendar year."

"That's all right. I just want to drive."

My only stipulation was no stops in Ho-Ho-Kus or Paramus. This did not prove too prohibitive in the eyes of the supervisor, who always had to stretch to cover the casino runs. I was hired.

The job came with a company-issued uniform, complete with sturdy, styleless shoes, which in my size had to be special-ordered. The line started me on major routes like Atlantic City and Foxwoods. My stomping grounds were the monotonous stretch of 95 through Connecticut and the Mobius run up and down Jersey's twin toll roads. I accepted almost any schedule, carried a cell, and made myself unconditionally available for substitutions. At the wheel, my hardy hands were happily without distractions, and the company kept me on the road every hour I wasn't sleeping.

I rented an apartment near one of the upstate terminals and it didn't make a difference whether it was Utica or Rome; it was just the dark intermission between successive trips: a futon, a shower, a microwave, a term, and a caveman named Merle crooning on the MP: "I'm on the run, the highway is my home."

It was wholesome work, as sincere as you could get, it appeared to me. Motor-coach operators were not superior men and women; we were diligent stewards of the people. For the first time I had the simple satisfaction, which to my sensibilities seemed perversely exotic, of earning an honest wage. I looked my passengers square in the face, whereas I had never locked gazes with any of my pocket patrons—this would have been against one of the cardinal rules of picking. I took their tickets, ripped, returned half, and riders and I imparted that instant of existential recognition that transcends all exertions of discourse, either oral, scriptural, or electronic. *Any open seat.* It was the moment that told them I knew where they were going and let me know they were satisfied I would take them there, one of the deep, ingenuous transactions that has not been bested by advances in global communication and virtual visitation, namely: the empirical drudgery of translating a body through space. Trafficking meat will never become obsolete. The numbing discomfort of the seats, the rubber fingertips of no-slip flooring grabbing shoe bottoms, the sickening smell of overheated cesspool seeping up the aisle from the john: These elements conspired to give us all—myself and my passengers, the mechanics and dispatchers, the fat-assed management who themselves flew first class—an abiding satisfaction that, however unpleasant, the safety of our passage was assured by the most rugged and rigorous mode of conveyance: the passenger bus, leviathan of the road.

I submerged memories of my former lives beneath devotion to my job. Movement occupied me, distance defined me. I measured the stretches, but not the time. If each mile corresponded more or less to a minute, it was only on some other, abstract plane that did not concern me. My heart beat in synch with the thunk of the highway joints. In my new vocation, I caught the eye of a maximum-capacity sixty-five persons four or five times a day. By and large, the sojourners who chose my coach hailed from a special milieu—more amorphous than stratum, somewhere not so much between as adjacent to the class divisions of those who went by automobile, rail, sea, and air. My passengers were prone to motion discomfort or afraid to fly; they had seen too many derailment picts or had never learned how to drive. The bus is a great leveler. The people who take it just want to go big red, leave their lovers, leave the driving to us. I could tell by the volume of baggage and the length of time they lingered on the platform bidding good-byes whether it would be a long absence. On night runs, I observed their overhead-illuminated faces, twice reflected between black windows and my mirror, looking out at a dark departure town for what might be the last time. Over extended flights of frivolity, I waxed sanguine and imagined that I was ferrying, among the anonymous bodies who had stepped up from the platform, my actual parents. Anything was possible, I tried telling myself, even that the detestable mayor and his sexy wife were not Dad and Mom. But I wasn't kidding anybody. Deep inside, I knew such delusions had to do with an addiction to running, a dependency which heightened my capacity for fantasy.

I was still Fast Eddie, although on a different scale from that of the early days. Turnpike, Parkway, Thruway, Connector, Expressway, and Interstate were my sprinting grounds. I could do Newark to Atlantic City in an hour, New York City to Stonington in just under two. Troopers across three states had heard of Fast Eddie but had never seen him in action. My method? It was partly that I did not strive. It didn't require any highfalutin system, radar scanning, or channelling nineteen for smokies. Rather, there was a Zen to it like that of wallet-lifting: slipping by like you belong, bolting through like lightning, and for the love of Pete, never—especially when encountering a surprise speed trap—slowing up or otherwise exhibiting signs of culpability. By no means did I exceed the limit all the time. In fact, a lot of days I was just on time. Some foolhardy scofflaws made it a point of pride: "I can't drive" fifty-, seventy-, or ninety-five. My credo: "Excess in moderation." I had a sort of sixth sense for correct conditions. Although dispatchers, drivers, mechanics, luggage-handlers, and ticket-sellers built up the hype around my every arrival, my own satisfaction was purely personal. If by extension I could steal a little extra time off the trip table, all the better. This was my sublimated subversion, the vicarious vent for all the criminal energies of my upbringing. In the treacherous trousers of the Northeast known as the tri-state area, the great highways were as pockets, and my shuttle snaked through folds and furrows like a slick, steely finger, every day's record time better than a fat billfold packed with cabbage.

I tried to convince the regular passengers that my good fortune was limited purely to the fact that I never got stopped, but they never believed me. They were ball-spinners, crapshooters, slot-feeders, and card-counters caught up in blackjack, pai gow, jacks-or-better, and all the video variations. Occasionally, one would cajole me into sitting on his lucky side during a poker hand, calling red or black while the wheel reeled in its hypnotic roulette, touching dice before a loaded throw, or pulling the bandit's solitary arm. It never lasted long. Invariably, I broke out in a drenching sweat and the gamblers discovered there was no such luck in these big bones.

I never once approached Ho-Ho-Kus, charting its position only by the stars, but on my constant runs I obtained occasional news of the one-time hometown from papers, passengers, and Net, as well as from that anarchic and, when it comes to deregulated democracy of discourse, as-yet-unbested medium known as citizens' band. Pauly, after conducting searches, offering rewards, and, with a glimmer of intuition that impressed me despite my contempt, having the Hackensack and Saddle Rivers dredged, gave up searching and admitted to the press that I had been "a little wild." Shots of the first lady crying in the tabloids were more than I could bear to look at. Merry kept herself busy as den mother of a local boy scout troop. While it broke my heart to have left her in the lurch, I never dared drop the Correntes a line, lest I alert Apple Jack's intelligence to an opportunity at following through on his shadowy threats. The PR from the whole melodrama of find-ing their prodigal son only to lose him again just served to boost the mayor's approval rating among his sympathetic citizens, and Pauly's re-election meant he must have managed to remain in the Jersey crime boss's favor. There had been no reprisals from the despot, so I figured I had done the right thing by staying away from Ho-Ho-Kus. The only times I ever ventured near the town where my parents laid their heads was when I blew by on the Turnpike at ninety miles per hour.

While I was making my monotonous runs up and down the Parkway and I-95, Apple Jack went semi-legit. The penny arcade proprietor, by his ruthless influence, had shored up city after city like so many big-boy toys until he called the shots throughout the entire northeast corridor. He rode his golden chariot up to Mass and ran for mayor of the Beast. Throughout the campaign, Apple Jack expertly affected the whole baby-kissing routine. Most people thought of him as an enormous teddy bear with a smile of genuine gold, and so the city council shrugged when Apple Jack stole the election. He kept up the gentle giant charade during his first months in office, but those of us familiar with Bean Town politics weren't fooled. Apple Jack was affecting the patina of public figure because he knew how the city's strong-mayor system worked: The initial term is going steady, the second is the wedding, and from there on out it's pure honeymoon. Fossilized leaders like White, Flynn, Menino, and so on had each gone a decade or more in this town-without-term-limits, invincible demagogues running unopposed or against token challengers, flexing their muscles all the way. If Apple Jack managed to get re-elected twice, his awful gravity would become the biggest new force the Beast had seen since the turn of century 21. Someday, he would cause more trouble than both the Bolger brothers put together. In the meantime, Mayor Apple Jack remained the wicked witch rolled up inside the wizard.

It was an eventful age, but I managed to stay above it all—six feet above, to be precise. That's how high my ass was perched above macadam. Riding a few heads over automobile roofs was like jumping to a transcendental place with perspective beyond the realm of regular mortals. I knew all those cars were down there, and I was careful not to squash them. Meanwhile, my army of sundry defeated passengers and I shot back and forth between marble palaces on purposeful missions, even if my purpose was only the back-and-forth. It was not a little unnerving, piloting a chrome shuttle over worse-than-lunar surfaces, but it beat offing your father, effing your mother. I was in a good place, where I belonged. There was sanctuary in kinesis. The moving kept me safe. Above the mad, rattling gyre of sidewalks, streets, and doorways, a sober judiciousness reigned. Without slowing down, there was no way that lust and murderous musing could catch up with me.

The months ticked away like numbers on a doctored odometer. On those long, ludicrous runs, I had a lot of time to think under the mantric influence of passing lamps and the Om-like drone of downshifting. I was a mariner on a sea of the fragrant hydrocarbons in ebb and flow with carbon-monoxide, which has no odor. In no small measure intoxicating, albeit highly toxic, on a cold winter day the bouquet of engine exhaust fills the lungs with the artificial afterburn of pious, if poisonous, warmth, and in the heat of summer offers an almost mentholated chill to nostrils, sinuses, and cerebellum. I hear synapses shut down like circuits extinguished by a dry spike of frost: *snik!* Yes, I allowed myself to become a bit fritzed by this noxious routine, and I did not fail to recognize an element of self-cancellation in all the headlong-rushing toward the next (or, as the Buddhists would have it, my chance at escaping the wheel of this same) world. I entertained reincarnation as an opportunity to clear the slate, reboot the system. Next time, I would hang onto that umbilical real tight and not let the culprits out of my sight. I never did get rid of my morose fascination with death, although it lay dormant, certainly, all the time I had other lives in my hands; this was perhaps my surest insurance, although every morning I was horrified by the prospect of being left to return an empty bus at the end of the day: What enticing voices might attend such a star-crossed mission?

Every so often, a schedule would take me into the Beast. I might have tried to look up Shep, except I never touched the ground. For a driver involved in the swift evacuation and replenishment of passengers, the Hub hardly ever felt like a real destination. Ramps removed coaches right up to the fourth-story terminal and deposited them back on the highway without ever allowing a wheel to tread the surface of the city.

In the South Station waiting area, I bumped into all sorts of hard-luck weirdos. On one shuttle run to East Beast, I was talking current events with an old-timer, a one-hundred-year-old flower child, health nut, conspiracy theorist, and compulsive gamble, who had been riding right up front for as long as I had been driving. He was always holding forth on one or another social subject, and this time he filled me in on the underground siege. The subterranean revolution had been blockaded by a traitor, one of their own who had bugged out. Miss Spinks, the transvestite hacker and chief of underworld security, had scrambled the passwords for the seven entrances to the submerged colony and holed herself up in the sewers, leaving Dig City inhabitants trapped inside, stuck without any means of procuring provisions from above. The psychotic Spinks had reprogrammed the security codes in the central artery's old command bunker: the Pan-Harbor Operations Command and Infrastructure Service. While she played VR and smoked too much loco weed, Dig City waited out starvation or suffocation.

"Sounds like just a stoner bent on sabotaging the co-op from his little hacker hole," I said.

"She's an anarchist and a Leo," annotated the centenarian bettor. "Wants to be unattached and in charge at the same time."

As I was pulling up to the casino in East Beast on the next-to-last leg of my run, the old-timer needled me for my zodiacal sign. I did not know, so I had to tell him the date. That very day turned out to be my twenty-first birthday, my real twenty-first birthday. "You mean to tell me you haven't taken a day off in almost five years, you've never gotten a ticket, never had an accident, and you just turned twenty-one?"

"I guess."

"Then you have got to let me buy you a drink—in the blackjack room."

I had an hour break so I went along, but we never got to the beverage. Poor guy, he busted every time. Even beginning with can't-lose combinations like ace-seven he managed to misplace his nerve and go over while the dealer held at seventeen. When he started holding low, the dealer trumped with blackjack. "I've never had such a bad streak!" he said. I was cold-sweating in that cavernous hall of clockless walls and perpetual fluorescence. It was not so much for any phobia of gambling, but of gamblers. Along with all the funny money, chips, and cheap buckets of slot feed, they frequently carried great wads of actual American cash. When I saw such bundles, my hands instinctively itched.

"I told you I wasn't lucky that way."

"Hey, you don't look so good, Eddie. Maybe you should get some fresh air."

"I better get back to the bus."

A half-hour remained until departure and I decided to buy myself a birthday beer at the Crossroads Tavern, a worried way station beneath the casino for the losers, the non-players, and the weary coach operators. I found the place agreeable at first dreary, inky light. The karaoke machine in the corner was dusty with disuse. Someone had finger-traced desolate letters in the coating of crud: "Long live the King." I liked my first beer after just one sip from the greasy mug. I was beginning to think this might be the beginning of a beautiful dependency when a madman burst into the bar with all the ceremony of a psychopathic slug. "Arise! Beastonites!" he howled in maniacal half-laughter.

With rings on all his fingers, the leather-suited stranger couldn't be a complete hound. One thing I noticed right away: He was wearing a really nice watch. A pimp? A nightclub singer? A high-class huckster? A furloughed schizophrenic? The retinue at his coat tails seemed to belie this last guess. They were not the clinical type: five guys, mirrorshaded goons in dark suits with conspicuous ear pieces, the signal features of those security automatons typically managed by an unseen genius. Two shadowed the mac daddy's every move while three others hovered at the door.

I pushed the glass back towards the well and was swallowing my last mouthful of sour brew when a meaty clap on my back caused me to sputter. What little beer did not get sucked into my lungs sprayed across the bar top. "Another round for the birthday boy," the buffoon bellowed into my ear for all the bar to hear. A grievous glance broke the bad news: to my right, the only empty seat.

The blue, boozy equilibrium of the heretofore maudlin tavern had been upset and everyone peered uneasily over their beers, glaring sideways not at him but at me, as if I had betrayed them by involuntarily invoking this insufferable extrovert. I was using my tie to mop the suds from my chin when I had a strange feeling and mouthed, almost unconsciously, and, I believed, inaudibly, "How did you know—?"

"Relax!" the bumptious intruder growled, climbing up on the stool beside mine. I had barely fed him his cue and he was already stepping on my lines. "It's everyone's birthday when the King sits down beside them!"

This so-called King was swarthy and the gray had just begun to streak his temples. He was not stoned, per se, but his eyes—great, broad oculars with dilated pupils—suggested he was soused on something, probably a lot of things: a stiff cocktail of cybertropics blended with a volatile mix of delusions and topped with a twist of overripe ego. My eye on his timepiece, I was idly contemplating a snatch and dash, but a surreptitious look toward the exit told me that was not an option. One of the not-so-secret servicemen posted at the door shook his head in definitive defiance. Sure enough, I was going to have to ride this one out to some kind of climax. This was what happened when a person with my luck entered a bar.

The bartender placed a yard-long stein before me. I thought for a moment that it was just for show. There could be no way to lift such a thing to one's lips—the fluted stem stretched almost all the way to the ceiling of that dank, airless saloon—but upon lowering my gaze along the entire amber length, eyes settled on the little apparatus at the base, a sort of nozzle made out of surgical tubing. I had heard of this: beer bong.

"Look," I said, "I don't drink."

"Oh yeah," he said, motioning to the measly glass I had just drained, verily dwarfed by the brimming monolith beside it, "what do you call that?"

I thought I might appease him by drawing a little draught, but before I could try a bejeweled hand had covered the mouth of my pudgy mug. "Oh no you don't. This little piggy," he said, fondling the thing's spigot, "goes between your lips."

The goon at our star's right shoulder cracked a sadistic grin, but Barrymore himself beheld my dilemma with perfect, ingenuous earnest: The kook really believed it was in the interest of fun, and failed to detect any signal whatsoever of my own disenchantment. Patrons who moments before had brooded agreeably over their stale distillations became inebriated by the air of imminent punishment. They shuffled over and crowded around with glasses raised to watch how their former fellow in erstwhile self-absorption would be served up. As a newcomer, I had trespassed, however innocently, by raising this evil spirit. A pink pique of bloodlust came to a hundred-some eyes marbled with over-indulgence and under-sleep. Recognizing at that instant the presence of all the elements for a precipitate of dark crowd pathology, I resigned myself to the instigator's unctuous injunction.

"Show 'em, son!" he cried, pounding the top of the bar. I sucked down the sparkling gall in great, convulsive gulps.

"Bring it home, son!"

Finished, I roared a great, curdling burp.

My captor swaggered over to the karaoke corner and picked up the microphone. "Ever have a woman treat your heart cruel?" he announced to the roomful of brutes, eliciting an approbatory murmur.

"Did you ever come home from working hard, traveling far, and your baby's wearing that loved-on look?" A grumble went up indicating general empathy.

"When that kind of thing happened to the King, I'd say, 'That's all right mama.'"

He shook a hip. There were cheers, whistles.

"I'd say, 'You're just a natural-born beehive, filled with honey to the top.'"

Hoots and hollers.

"You know what I'd say? 'Hey mama, don't you treat me wrong. Come and love your daddy all night long.' That's what I'd say."

Howls, snorts.

"But she's a stingy little mama, 'bout to starve me half to death. So you know what I told her? 'I'm leaving town, baby. I'm leaving town for sure.'"

Foot stomping, bar banging.

"That big eight-wheeler runnin' down the track means your true lovin' daddy ain't a-comin' back." A general yee-haw.

"Move on ol' son, move on!" The self-proclaimed King lowered his sunglasses a touch and peered over the frames with icy blue eyes. "Only thing is, friends, what could I say to my boy?"

People piped down.

"I stood over his crib. 'You're sleeping son, I know, but, really, this can't wait. I wanted to explain—before it gets too late . . . ' " He tilted the glasses back and flicked a switch on the karaoke machine. Sentimental strings swelled shrilly from the speakers. Words scrolled across the screen and the man sang:

For your mother and me, love has finally died.
This is no happy home, but God knows how I've tried.

All sniffed over their snifters, sobbed into their bottles, and glugged in their mugs. There wasn't a dry martini in the house.

The surly sadist came back over to my spot. "You ever consider," he whispered in my ear, "how no animal but man has the genius to kill himself? Human beings are the only species intelligent enough to consider taking their own lives."

"But we're not the only ones," I said with a hiccup.

"Among lemmings it's just a lark," the snake hissed in earnest, "a symptom of their legendary impressionability—not glimmerings of real genius. A man, on the other hand, knows every moment it's up to him to get it over with."

I was thinking: I get it, a comedian of despair. He liquors me up to offer this ontological one-liner. What he did not know was that the gag was wasted on me. Not only was I not wowed by the ixnay-Homo sapien routine, I would have gladly persuaded him that he was right. Besides butchering the little he had probably picked up in a Philosphy-101 semantics course, he had accomplished nothing but invocation of an easy truism: The question is *why not die?*, not *why go on?*

A shriek from my pocket—I fumbled with the cell. It was the dispatcher. "You have to bring your coach back to the yard. Make it fast, Eddie."

"But my return passengers," I blubbered into the phone.

"Another driver has already been sent for the next leg. Get that bus back here, now." The dispatcher hung up.

I felt woozy, but my cynical tormentor had challenged me on personal turf, and he had made one assumption that could not be left tacit. I clutched his wrist and whispered, "Not lemming: Apis mellifera, the honey bee—particularly the female, or worker, of the species. Hers is a noble suicide. When she gives up her one-and-only sting, she's a goner. It's self-sacrifice for the sake of the hive."

Ashen, no longer so smug, the joker replied, "That is, presuming she knows she's going to die."

The expandable metal band was a worthy challenge. It would have been easier with a buckle or clasp. "Bees know. It's probably a collective superconscience that makes them do it—that's what the scientists say. Hell, they wittingly rip their little asses in half. Anything to protect the queen." Shakily, I stood. "Look, pal, it's been nice talking to you, but I really have to go. That was the boss on the phone. My bus has been called back to the yard."

He patted my ass. "Taking the TW?"

"It's the only way to Southie."

I walked past the guards and out of the bar with a decent

counterfeit of an expensive Swiss wristwatch in my pocket. When the King ordered his next drink, I bet he still felt the ghost impression of my grip on his naked wrist.

I lingered ten minutes in the terminal, offering to pay passersby for accompanying me on the quick trip to the Southie yard, but it was no use. I had to get on an empty bus. I was buzzed, and I had to pilot myself alone on this brief excursion that would seem, I could foresee, like a tunnel of infinity. I pulled out my key chain and absently patted my pocket, but the familiar bulge was not there. It took a second, along with the recognition of what it was like to feel blitzed, to realize that, while I had been busy snatching his watch, the creep had lifted my wallet. In my first day of adult life, a flamboyant casino thief had outsped Fast Eddie. Ha! That buffoon had relieved me of the hallmark of my family history, that billfold of Corrente leather. The larcenist's services had come cheaply, as far as I was concerned. I had his timepiece and he had my wallet, but he had done me a favor by taking that wretched thing. Hopefully he was on his way to enjoying a meal on my last week's pay, the fruit of maybe a dozen runs up the parkway and through the thruway, runs I would rather forget, anyway. That wallet had been the weight which kept me biting my tongue while lugging old ladies' bags full of grief and listening to sorry suckers' war stories about one-armed bandits. What a peculiar sensation overtook me on that, the night of my twenty-first birthday. I had been unburdened of the weight that had kept me bound to Pauly all these years. Pulling out of that parking area, I felt ready for anything. Without a history, I was in the hands of destiny.

The global positioning system told me there were no other

cars heading into the Ted Williams tunnel toward Chinatown. I was alone on the narrow, two-mile, monotonous shot under the harbor. Half-consciously, I began accelerating. Eighty. All that would be required was a flick of the switch back to manual and a nudge of the wheel—not even a turn, just a tap. Ninety. Spinning out upon contact with the wall and violently wedging itself sideways inside this narrow tube, the chassis would snap and the body would explode like a five-ton marshmallow entering the earth's atmosphere from outer space. One hundred miles per hour. Chunks of bus and pieces of me would paint the curved surfaces with strokes of blue flame. "ATTENTION: TUNNEL UNDER VIDEO SURVEILLANCE" —someone would get to appreciate the incendiary display.

I was wrested back to reality when the global positioning system beeped and a blip appeared on the screen. I had company: another vehicle, a heavy one, coming down the TW from the opposite end, a dump truck or possibly a long-bed. I took my foot off the pedal, relieved to no longer be alone with my neurosis, and flicked the citizens' band on nineteen. Right away came a standard salutation: "Breaker one-nine: Can I get a radio check?" The voice sounded familiar, but maybe it was just because of the generic Southern drawl people assume on CB.

"Ten-four. Got you loud and clear. Over."

"What's your handle, partner?"

"Fast Eddie."

"Fast Eddie the bus driver?"

"That's a ten-four."

"What's your forty?"

"Southbound in the TW. What's your handle, buddy?"

"This is the King . . . " That's when I recognized the voice:

It was the same sicko who had harassed me in the bar. Right before I had been bound by my occupation to take a ride through the deserted gauntlet, he had gotten a kick out of telling me his underwhelming theory on self-annihilation, snatched my wallet, and made his getaway through the tunnel. While I dawdled in the terminal, he had decided to turn back and taunt me some more. Now, on the squawk box, he was trying to run me off the road with more moribund logic: "About those bees: You know who runs the hive? The queen. What happens to the drone? After a while, the workers drag him out of the nest, and if he tries to crawl back he gets ripped apart."

"Sure wish I could stay and chit-chat, King, but you're breaking up. Over and out."

I shut the radio off thinking, easy, E, you can shake this. The line of lights on the tunnel walls whizzed by hypnotically and I set the steering on automatic. The GPS screen made me think the system was off kilter, so I gave the dashboard a whack, but the apparition of high-beam headlights confirmed the incredible data. The King was headed right down the middle of the narrow tunnel, as if he had sighted his hood ornament smack on the double line. I honked. I flashed. I sent a distress ping via the collision-avoidance system, but it was no use, the psycho kept speeding towards me in the center of the two-lane death trap. There was no telling what kind of cargo he might be carrying, but as components for a pipe bomb our empty craft alone accounted for more than thirty-thousand pounds of mostly steel and three hundred gallons of volatile fuel. It was a mile behind me to the mouth, I was stuck like a caramel nut cluster right in the pit of the Inner Harbor's large intestine, and here came a ten-ton enema. Gears grinding, axles shrieking, brakes nevertheless did not squeal.

There was a quarter mile between the speeding juggernaut and my bus and ten seconds left until impact. I went slack in the driver's seat, blazing headlights blinding my sight. What was it in those shining eyes that seemed to be watching me and watching themselves watching me at the same time? Maybe it was the overriding madness of the King, a suicide in overdrive. Exhilarated, with perhaps a hundred yards to go in this murderous game of chicken, I was awakened to an overwhelming, alien impulse: the will to live. I stomped on the emergency brake and, the coach skidding and kicking up a great plume of vaporizing rubber, jumped up in my seat and popped the seal on the driver's emergency window. No! I would not go!—at least not gently.

I dove, rolled, cradled my head against the mammoth blast, and was blown away—right down an uncovered manhole. Weirdly, I did not hit bottom. The walls coddled me, a plummeting Alice, and cushioned my fall. My body came to rest in the oozy abdomen of the under-tunnel. Glasses still sat snug on my nose, but I could not see. In a dumbfounded crouch I kept checking and rechecking myself for injuries, finding none. Was this what it was like to be dead? The kamikaze's watch pecked at my left wrist, an instantaneous reminder of the intercourse that had just rocked my otherwise imperturbable indifference. The antique timepiece was still ticking off the last time he gave it a wind. I tried the tiny light— it worked. As if in response, right in front of me, a hatch opened onto an unseemly, unsanitary hovel.

The air was redolent with incense whose smoke seemed at

once exotic and familiar, the cavern dimly lit by too many monitors flashing fragmented images from every corner. Walls were bathed by a cathode glow. Idols glinted in the unearthly light. In the center of it all loomed a gargantuan she-bulk in Buddha-like pose, meaty hands working some kind of ritual accessory at her lap—dharma balls? prayer beads? At the heart of the eerie tableau, on the apex of the Fury's lotus, what beamed most bluely beneath a beehive of peroxide locks was a great, round, lunar face, as remote and inviolable as an Indonesian death-mask, features frozen as if in a trance. From what I could tell, her fat, fulsome belly, bulging out of a triple-extra-large Philadelphia Eagles T-shirt, melted into the lion-skin-covered couch.

She cried, "Sheeeee-itfuck! Goddamn zombies gone and robbed my high score!" then saw me and said, "Lights! Music!"

The room exploded with a fluorescent ferocity that made me cover my eyes in reflex. Blaring out of unseen amplifiers, old-time hip-hop music of the gangsta variety caused me to shift my monkey-see-no defense to my ears. When finally I could peer squintingly about, a quick glance to the monitor at my back revealed the source of her momentary consternation: GAME OVER. There was no discernible exit. The door had swallowed me up and closed behind me. Whose hideous indignation had I invoked by my inadvertent audience?

"Relax!" said the great diva, nested in the midst of a patch of throw pillows. She had put down her joystick and was occupied with a task on the table between us, fiddling with a see-through cylinder that reminded me of the stein the suicidal maniac had earlier made me chug. "Play a game or two. I've got all the best shoot-'em-ups." With the same, sickly light that had shone on me my first morning in Ho-Ho-Kus, I realized precisely who she was: the Brutus in drag who had master-minded the embargo on Dig City. Man! had I made a wrong turn! My slack jaw must have let leak the awestruck spurt, *it's Spinks*, because, bad breath blasting down from her great, huffing exhaust pipe of a mouth, she said, tickling my chin, "Miss Spinks to you."

I examined the hardware along the dark, dingy walls. The hacker's hideout, tucked away in an alcove of the TW deep beneath the mud of Inner Harbor, had been the control center for all the central artery tunnels. All of the underground infra-structure linked into here: access, surveillance, drainage, and ventilation. Spinks had decorated her bunker with the kitschi-est knick-knacks and pimpiest bits of mid-to-late century 20: lava lamps, black-light posters, rotating disco balls, pink fur upholstery, porcelain puppies with sad, bobbing faces. If it were found by a tacky enough collector, the lot would have fetched a fortune at an antique show.

I got the visceral sense that neither the climate nor the company were so good for my health. "I'm really sorry I burst in on you like this. Can I go now?"

"Not so fast," she said, narrowing her eyes. "You done trespassed." Monitors lighted up all over. Yikes! There was my bus on TV. I had been surveilled.

"But it was a mistake. I didn't mean to bother you."

She examined the compiled clips. "Hm, it sure does look that way." The speed, the swerving, the ejection—mercifully, Spinks stopped the replay before the crash. "Tell you what: We'll play a little game. If you win, I let you go."

"Please, Miss Spinks. . ."

"Aw, cut the sympathy shit," she interrupted, in a voice that, preternaturally resonant, did not need raising to be heard, and, tilting the barrel of a five-foot-long glass tube in my direction, added, "have a hit." Spinks packed the bowl at the crux of her cross-legged slouch with a plug of indistinguishable herb. She thrust the water pipe's weighted base my way, pushing aside the tabletop clutter of ashtrays, half-empty cans, obscure game controllers, and smoking paraphernalia.

"No, thanks. I'm, uh, nice."

"Go on. You're going to need it. This game's a bitch." As for the chiba, what could I do but draw a deep draught? So far, this invitation had been my only favorable sign.

My eyes began to adjust as the peculiar smoke affected my senses. Attached to Spinks's mainframe, a double saddle girthed a contraption on a cowish chassis. "Christ!" I cried—something about being high made me invoke odd gods—"it's a mechanical bull."

"That, my lass," Miss Spinks said, effortlessly lifting me off the floor and settling me in the front stock, "is my ass."

Mounted on the digital donkey, feeling fey and bold from the intoxicating smoke and the seeming ease of our interaction, I had to laugh.

Spinks's hot breath blasted in my ear: "It may seem funny, Eddie, but it ain't no joke. If you win, I take a dive. But if you fuck up, I cut your throat." Spinks raised a steely blade, long and curved. The edge gleamed unmistakably keen, although at the tip its luster was dulled by a brown coat of what might have been rust. How had she known my name? It was enough to make a neurotic with a belly full of beer become downright paranoid, but then white noise came blaring over the sound system and shortly I understood. Spinks had sampled the tunnel video feed as well as my CB exchange with the King. I had to hear it all over again, and queasily I marveled at how I had ever been capable of empathy for such a pretentious death rap. Now that I had narrowly, hairily escaped what might have been my nearest brush with elective death, I found myself in the clutches of a genocidal hacker and fiercely clinging to life.

I was altogether shaken now. "You see, Miss Spinks. That's why I don't smoke! I'm prone to paranoia anyway, and—"

"Don't sweat it, Eddie. Hit start."

The digital donkey began gently pumping and started over a hilly competition course. From the crown-wearing avatar on the wall-mounted monitor, I understood that I was king, and behind sat my queen, as played by Spinks. Data readouts: miles, lives, jackass points. The power glove on my right hand force-fed back the pressure of a bridle.

By mile five I could feel the beast teething the bit. "Wow," I said, my stoned guard lowered—I didn't even know I was speaking out loud, "nice code!"

"I programmed it myself. Wait'll you hit seven, where the ass starts kicking." By the time we made it to the ninth mile, the burro was really bucking. Spinks wrapped her elbow around my neck, raised her razor talon to the top of my throat, and spat, "A king and queen ride the jackass ten miles to the throne."

I almost lost my mount. "I can't see." I said, sucking air. Infinitesimally, Spinks loosed the grip.

"It's a riddle, bitch. Answer it."

"Oh, man," I moaned. On the monitor, there appeared in the distance what looked like an ocean liner. It had to be significant, as it was the first thing to show up on the horizon at the actual vanishing point of this tunnel-vision game. *A king and queen ride the jackass ten miles to the throne.* "A buh- . . . a buh- . . . a buh-. . . ."

"A whuh?"

The sweat streaking down my leg reminded me I had to pee. The basin shape on the monitor had made me think boat, but as it grew larger in the center of the enormous screen it looked more like a conical castle, immaculate white walls spreading outwards as they reached for the sky. *A king and queen ride the jackass ten miles to the throne.* "A cah- . . . a cah- . . . a cah- . . . ."

"Hunh?"

The curved knife pressed at my throat as parapets gleamed like porcelain. Porcelain parapets? Spinks was a better programmer than this. She would have texture-mapped the battlements. And why the funny, infunicular shape? Something about it reminded me of the pants I had just wet. *A king and queen ride the jackass ten miles to the throne.* "I think I've got it—!"

The last thing I saw before passing out: Miss Spinks hulking in the reflection of the monitor, eyes upon me piercingly, raising the razor with a bloodthirsty grimace. GAME OVER.

The ceiling was flickering blue. It must have been from all the empty screens. Where was she? I tried to sit up, but something rigid and cold about my waist barred erection. I kept calm by reminding myself that I was an escape artist: I would likely be able to wrest free, whatever the restraints. While attempting to roll over, I realized that it was no longer a saddle beneath me, but a softer, suppler seat. Wrapped in lion-skin print: the harpy's magnificent abdomen. The late Miss Spinks held me in her tender, ultimate embrace. I don't recall whether I raised my voice in protest when the walls came down, but come down they did. A bunch of SWAT-style oddballs burst in and, swarming around the mess, labored to pry me out of Spinks's mortal grip. As the lights went out a second time for me, I mumbled incoherently, "A royal flush."

When I came to I was slumped in a white chair in front of a white desk inside a white, windowless box before the whitest man I had ever seen. He wasn't an albino, just someone who had not gotten any sun for a long, long time. Light came from no perceptible source, glowing perhaps from phosphorous in the paint. I looked around for the hidden camera, which could not be detected, but whose invisible presence I unmistakably, electronically sensed. The walls and ceilings were bare. Far off, there was a sound like a fresh load dropping in the belly of an automatic ice-making machine.

"Who are you?" said the pale interrogator.

"Nobody."

"Don't give me that Odysseus bullshit. Your hands are soft. You've got a lot of pigment in your skin so you've must have a job up above. Where do you come from?" said the bleached bully.

"I've been trying to figure that out myself. Where am I?"

"You're in the Hive, headquarters for Dig City, dumbass."

"The name's Eddie."

"That's better. I'm Cray, second-in-command of the underground empire. Now, what were you doing trying to penetrate our periphery?"

Street stories had always made this place sound like a romantic world of diligence and determinism, and here I was in the blanched heart of it enjoying an audience with a washed-out bureaucrat. "I just dropped into a duct. I wasn't trying to penetrate anything."

"Listen here, Edgy, overworld agencies may call us subversives, but we're only down here to spurn the surveillance and computer networks they use to scan every action of the defeated, yea-saying, conformity-bent society upstairs. It's our inalienable right to be indistinguishable, and so we hold the tunnels." I thought someone should remind Cray that his whole scruffy cooperative had been held hostage by a lone, disgruntled hacker, but his delusion was not mine to disabuse. "Of course, we're left pretty vulnerable to demented drones like Miss Spinks. However clumsy your impregnation, Eggy, you just managed to save the movement." Pushing a piece of paper across the desk at me, Cray said, "This is the Dig City immigration form. Fill it out completely and we'll consider your status."

I had won Spinks's game and she had reopened the gates to Dig City. Now they wanted me to be their first new customer. "That's very kind of you, Mr. Cray, but I'm not certain I actually want to immigrate."

"You don't get it, do you? You already have. You're *here*.

Your current classification is illegal, as a matter of fact. Hero or no, you barged through our borders."

"But it was an accident."

"Involuntary impregnation? You think US Gov's INS would buy that? Come on! Take this form to your cell and we'll put it before naturalization in the morning."

A contingent of border patrol agents, the same thugs who had wrested me out of Spinks's death clutch, appeared in pale gray uniforms. Drunk, stoned, enervated, what could I do but endure the compulsory hospitality?

I was assigned to a compact domicile. They called it a cell, but not in the prison sense. Constructions of papier-mâché over chicken wire formed compartments along tunnel walls like the reticulated cells of a honeycomb. Walls were bare, furnishings spare, and the low ceiling left space to stand up but not to stretch arms overhead. Using the narrow bed as a bench, I pulled down a little ledge from the opposite wall. There was a keyboard built into one end and a little monitor imbedded in the wall. In order to stand up, I had to close the improvised desktop. In Dig City, I surmised, problems were worked out more or less horizontally.

I sat staring at the information form for a whole hour. And then another. I had been left empty by the Spinks ordeal and shell-shocked by the hara-kiri King, but I would have to make up a good story or the fanatics who ran Dig City might never let me leave. Without my wallet, I did not have the Swift ID on me, but I would never say Corrente. Even if I told my birthplace and date, it would be just as good as surrendering the surname. Since that run-in with Apple Jack at Adelle's, I had resolved not to imperil my parents. I had been lucky to make my getaway from the arcade without getting them in a mess of trouble, but if I ended up in the news, even from afar, I knew I could be the death of Pauly and totally screw over Merry. They thought I was dead, and that was for the best.

There was a rap at the door of my cell. It was a pale, homely lady from immigration. Sitting there in the little cubicle with the work ledge down gave me all the semblance of a busy and productive member of this bastard community, and you would think she would be impressed to meet the genius who had defeated the transvestite menace, but she just frowned and said, "So you don't have to go around looking like a bus driver." She tossed a change of clothes on the cot and left.

I traded my grubby driver's uniform for gray fatigues and lay down to try to sober up. I found my attention straying to ceiling and floor, wondering whether air ducts might swiftly dispatch me from this new indenture to Cray and his cracked cadre. I puzzled out the opportunities for escape: Spend a few days in this arrogant underground, pretend enthusiasm for the revolution, and then slip out through the sewage system, for instance. Although the bus was toast and the wallet had been lifted, my career profile was looking up. If I managed to get out and up and come back to life above as Eddie Swift, I would have a good alibi at the company's inquiry: "Abducted by underground crazies!" It would make a great tabloid headline. Besides, I could always get a job with one of the rival lines. I had met enough operators in diners and filling stations for references. Now that I was actually of eligible age, all I had to do was replace the ID and I was in like Flynn.

Another knock and I thought it must be the disdainful matron back to harass the captive rescuer, but when I opened the door I was blinded by an apparition of underground loveliness. Radiant at the entrance to my cell stood an ivory Aphrodite. Fair features struck me as somehow familiar. I rubbed my eyes and focused on her porcelain forehead: escaping from under her infantry cap, a single brunette curl made a boldface, upside-down question mark.

"Are you Freddie?"

"Yes," I said. "I mean, Eddie."

"I'm Jocy." The first lady of Dig City removed her cap and a great cascade of black hair spilled over her shoulders like the confluence of two dark, mysterious rivers. "Would you like to come to the canteen with me?" she said.

Was this just a joke, the cruel caricature of kindness towards the scorned stowaway? Although still sore from Cray's party-line spanking, I would not turn Jocy down. She was older than me, maybe forty—a sexy forty—but with a delicate complexion preserved by sequester from the sun. For someone who was practically royalty, Jocy did not seem the least preten-tious nor, for that matter, very regal in bell-bottom jeans that flattered long legs and flared to the floor. I followed her through Dig City's corridors and silently imbibed delicate breezes that smelled of hyacinth and minerals.

Most of Jocy's subjects were nothing short of fluorescent. Latinos lost their fabulous tans, Asians faded ghostly gray, and while some Africans got blacker, most mellowed to a freckled, earthy brown. At the canteen, Jocy and I measured scoops of hot cocoa and dehydrated mini-marshmallows into earthen-ware cups, filling them up with steaming jets from a faucet. "The water flows from a hot spring," she said, "but simple necessities like light and air don't come naturally down here."

Jocy dipped her biscotti—real biscotti, looted from a North End factory at the beginning of the Great Devaluation and preserved in its original packaging—and took a bite. I endeavored to emulate her method, but the sagging wand all at once collapsed and fell to a flaccid heap on my slacks. My fly got splashed with a soggy umber splotch—and the liquid seeping through was fucking hot! I held tongue, lap, and pride while trying nonchalantly to mop up the slop with a napkin, Jocy delicately sipping and nibbling her own stash on the side. Mother Merry, I thought, would have liked Jocy a lot.

In the next tunnel over from the canteen, we sat beside each other on a bench in front of an old Norge coin washer, I with a standard-issue towel around my waist, bony knees awkwardly crossed, while on the other side of the circular glass pants twirled in their underwater dance. Jocy filled me in about Vitamin D supplements and long physical education sessions under sun lamps in the gymnasium Levis had constructed out of the four-lane tunnel. She had been born underground to one of the first subterranean squatters. Jocy had not realized she was different from most children, presuming all movies shot on the surface to be science fiction, until her fourth-grade English class read "All Summer in a Day." Bradbury's story had seemed like her own vivid, if plaintive, biography. When she came to understand that in fact the vast rind of the globe implied the existence of people who did not enjoy shelter from the fabled sun or unpredictable meteorology, Jocy was overwhelmed by a sense of pity. She became involved with politics at DCU and was elected student body president. This early experience with domestic diplomacy assured that, once she earned her bachelor's degree, she was destined for the executive staff, where she eventually married Levis, the maximum leader.

"By the way," I said, "where is the chief?"

Jocy shrugged. "Trying to get his head out of his ass somewhere. You would think Levis might have been at work on the Spinks crisis, but he goes on these benders and leaves Cray to runs things while he's away. What do you think of Cray?"

"Cray? He's a real son of a—"

"He's my brother by the way."

"—Gun."

When the dryer cycle was done, Jocy spared me the risk of fumbling with the machine and humiliating myself further there in my loincloth. Something happened when she removed the pants. A change took place. The cosmos shifted. A massive force stirred. In rats' days, the precocious, pre-teen obsession had always been with boobs, a phenomenon that was probably linked to the subconscious effects of the by-and-large milk-starved orphans making up our ranks. Nurturing the fixation was Shep, who, perpetuating his Mephistophelean masquerade, was always making great, cupping motions with his hands in mimed enthusiasm for gifted misses. I had played along, mostly as a token to my overall homogeneity scheme: anything I could do to eschew unnecessary attention that would run the risk of starting people harping on my feet. My lazy corroboration contributed to the discomfort when I finally had gotten a load of Merry. With my penchant for pessimistic prescience, I should have expected that the idle banter would come back to get me, although I had never known how I would end up. I was unable to discriminate between boys' town machismo and the leftover longing for the lady who made me, but in a second in that subterranean laundromat I sat absolved of all that and found myself staring right in the cloaked eye, the heavy-lidded talisman, of my salvation and exaltation. Instantaneously, all those elements of Jocy's appearance that just moments before had seemed merely attractive—the lean legs, the long black hair, the sinuous smile—became beacons of supernatural luminosity, all trained radiantly on the tight-packed, perky, perilous focal point against which I would gladly have my frigate dashed: her ass.

I never fathomed the marrow of that bland assessment, "ass man," until the moment when, drooping over the dryer, Jocy rooted my heart from under my ribs with her fantastic back hoe, and then—happy birthday!—not only did I understand, but I embodied, even exemplified, the concept. The buzz that overtook me that second was perilously exhilarating. An aching earnest came over me. Heart beat lustily. I was lucid, alert, understanding. Songs about fat-bottom girls I could not recollect ever having heard boomed clearly in my ears. Mind reeled with shamanistic visions. I thought I had learned everything there was to know about adulthood well before the time I had been christened Corrente, but now an entirely new aspect of maturity had been aroused from deep within my dormant deviance. Here I was, out of my pants, wrapped in only a flimsy towel, the finest lady under earth meanwhile bent boldly over the gaping mouth of the dryer.

Would that there had been a whole hamper full of slacks, shirts, and hard-to-spot socks caught in static-electrified crannies just out of reach, that she might have spent eternity in that position and left my ecstasy complete! By the time she came out, flushed, perspiring from the hot blast inside the tumbling chamber, I was a changed man. I was a man. Jocy turned away while I pulled on the trousers and slipped stiffness beneath the elasticized waistband.

Back in slacks, crisp and toasty, having regained a bit of composure, I walked Jocy back to her cell.

"You are very brave, Eddie, plunging right in with Miss Spinks."

"It was nothing," I stammered, "really. I didn't even know I was doing it 'til it was done."

"I hope there's some way we can repay you." Jocy's little alabaster hand, cool and smooth, brushed against the hair of my knobby knuckles and stoked a long-dormant longing. A bird leapt in my chest, fluttering. What was that dark stirring inside of me? "Sweet dreams, Eddie."

Back at my cell, I sat at the work ledge and wryly remembered Madame Adelle, Amazing Oracle. She had doubtless gotten a lot done out of her cramped cabinet over maybe two hundred years, so how could I complain about the confines of this cozy chamber? All through the night I seethed with my boner, postponing the inclination to dilute the purity of my revelation by taking the matter into my own hands. I exulted that a woman had distracted me from my Merry mortification. So what if Jocy was completely out of my league and married—

to the head honcho, no less? If I wanted the opportunity to see her again, my story had better be a good one.

Anyone who has gone straight through to dawn in a reverie lusting after someone new knows the attendant inspiration cannot be compared. Elated to be alive, I luxuriated in the simple, private satisfaction of connecting ideas and designs while assembling an artificial autobiography that I believed would satisfy the Dig City sentinels. Along with giving me a woody, Jocy had intimated a spin on Spinks and my stumble in: Play it off as a guerrilla action, not a monkey accident. It would do no good for them to make the connection to that tunnel crash, which must be all over the news. In tribute to the maniac trucker, I appropriated his handle for a surname: Eddie King. Haven't heard of me? Exactly. I claimed to be a VR jockey and Net hacker who specialized in security: cracking ice and leaving no trace. Spinks's game? I said I had pirated it from her mainframe and played it a thousand times before sneaking into her lair and winning big!

At dawn, a sumptuous fever brought on the fiercest of all primal impulses and thoughts returned to the monumental woman who had saved me from the mother of all complexes. Clasping the mental image of Jocy in bell-bottoms, I understood the lure of the sirens, the legendary allure of Circe. They had used a euphemism for Helen: It had not been her face that had launched those thousand ships. Here was what the poet pined over while he strummed his lyre, the reason for the chase, the battle, the sacrifice. I knew why the stallion reared for his mare, the dog bayed for his bitch, my hips distinctly twitched. I am animal! I am man! Batter me! Bash me! Capsize me! Bang me up against your hazardous reef!

In the morning I was summoned back to the Hive. Clutching my masterpiece of mythomania, I stalked the sloped streets of the underground city. By the time I arrived at that bleached monument of minimalism, I had a whole new attitude for a winning interview. I handed my immigration form over to the hag who had delivered my britches and was admitted to the empty Hive.

Waiting there in isolation, I was thinking about how nice it would be to stick around for a while. What if I could set up a solid life in Dig City as, say, a social philosopher, publishing gritty tracts for the local rags, perhaps settling down with a pretty little Pollyanna? Here I went, feeling all tender and earnest. To be part of a family! There were serious matters at hand—and I could be involved.

When it comes to technological progress, there is a sort of

societal yin and yang: entrepreneurs like myself whose ingenuity tends toward abstraction combined with those whose enterprises consist of concretion—in Pauly's case, excretion. While Pauly had made his billions at the rate of about a dollar per flush, I foresaw a future in more esoteric modes. Overnight, I had gotten an idea that the dynamos and generators of the overworld could adequately supply sufficient energy for every mole man, woman, and child. Dig City's current attitude was too frugal. Anyone could tell from the bounteous buzz of street lamps and the incessant hum of the MBTA's train lattice that there was more than enough juice.

I had expected to see Cray, but instead a drawn man in sunglasses entered and sat at a term. Instead of a regular monitor, it had a touch screen for Braille text and tactile tables. I was wondering who he was and whether he was aware that I was there when he sighed, as if reading my mind, "I'm the sorry sucker who gets to triage immigration applications." He lowered his shades to rub his eyes and I saw by the sockets that he was genuinely blind. You could tell by the burnt-out bulbousness. "My name's Terry, and I'm Dig City's Minister of Information. And you're Eddie King, who it just so happens got lucky and disarmed the time bomb ticking over this city for weeks."

Although I had already made up my mind to stay in Dig City, I figured I might as well play hard-to-get, a pose that had been denied me all those years as serf in one or another syndicate. "What's the big deal with information?" I challenged. "For a community founded on ideals of anonymity, you sure are keen on spying."

"What I do is not spying," he replied. "I prefer calling myself a seer. Let me tell you: What happened with Spinks could happen again. She was post-paranoid, period. Spinks thought everyone was out to get her, and she knew she was indestructible in that spot beneath the Ted Williams tunnel. If the riddle had been stored in any of her networked data, we would have cracked it, but Spinks knew that. She decided on a self-detonating technique that would let any lucky old schmo— uh, that is, hero—end her desolate siege." I was about to tell Terry that he was wasting his breath with the recruitment routine, that I had decided to stick around for a while, when the self-styled seer abruptly stood and two stony-faced guards entered. "Upon review of your immigration forms, it has been determined that you are unfit for citizenship."

My heart sank. "Why?"

"I haven't been able to verify your history. It was a hell of a night in Dig City. The Spinks thing was only half of it. There's a very fragile balance in the underground right now, and we can't take chances with rogue vigilantes. So long, Eddie King."

The guards holding my arms, I staggered through the main tunnel. Abject, abstracted, I retraced the dizzying sequence of steps that had propagated my enchantment with the under-ground mission. The process had involved several stages of shedding skepticism while reverting to an infantile submissive-ness before the domineering characters who ran Dig City. There had been something sisterly about the immigration matron's brusque down-dressing, a fraternal felicity to Cray's arm-twisting. As for Terry's tough-luck lecture, maybe this was the way you were supposed to feel when crying "uncle": bruised, bested, grateful to someone stronger than you, a little sadistic, who teased and tortured. I had not met such a compelling cast since the Nec, and I coveted their constraints. I wanted to be dominated, damn it!—at least in the sibling, simpatico sense. Perhaps it was not patrimony I had always been after, but just the simple, kindred Doppelgänger: a brother or sister to worship, burn out on, and spurn; someone to smack and, in turn, be smacked. Half a decade earlier, I had gotten labeled Corrente, and yet those parents had been unable to offer me what I really wanted: a kid brother, big sister, or just a cousin, inventoried but not indexed, caretaken but not taken care of. With such a kin to take care of me, I might not have become such a morose only child.

Above all, there was Jocy. Already I felt like I would not survive without seeing her again. As a bus driver, I had been smug about my alienation, but I had just been racing toward cold comfort. Now there was no way I could keep on a bee-line for geriatric days, hell-bent on a time and a frame of mind when it would not matter to me any more whether I ran, although I could not be certain if such a time would ever arrive. By displacing tits with ass, Jocy had substituted monarch for mom, and distracting me from my mother fixation she had given me a new reason to live.

Stupefied, I was brought to the northbound lanes beneath Dewey Square, the deepest point in all Dig City, where the entire colony had congregated, the pumped-in air buzzing with laughter and song. The central tunnel went down 120 feet to duck beneath three other levels—the Red Line, the Silver bus loop, and the lobby of Dewey Square station—then cut up in a five percent grade to cross over the Blue Line at about thirty-six feet before heading out the tunnel mouth to the cable stay bridge. By all of this dramatic digging, the abandoned artery had bequeathed Dig City an enormous hall of the people known in the underground as the Comb.

"You've got to wait before we can take you up," said the thug at my left shoulder. "There's a rally going on."

We stood up front near where Cray, at center stage, had his arms raised. "Stay calm," he shouted above the din. The people of Dig City would not pipe down. Voice cracking, Cray crowed, "I have everything under control."

Catcalls, whistles—somebody called, "Give us the gamer!" Others in the crowd began taking up the cry: "We want the King kid!"

Scowling, Cray came over and grabbed my arm. "This happens every now and then. You can't control them. Looks like you're up, Eddie."

Cray yanked me toward the middle and the swarm began to settle. Did lucky breaks come in threes? Hell, I sure hoped so. Anyway, it had been that way back when I had sucker-punched Some Nerd, escaped a mother's bosomy headlock, and head-faked Apple Jack all in one night. Now after the TW squeeze and the Spinks tour, I was going to get a last-ditch grip on Dig City. I looked out at the swelling sea of pale faces and prepared to plumb my submerged powers of performance. It was just like back in the day of the old sideshow, only instead of begging for attention from a handful on the sidewalk, I would be up there locus solis, front and center. Whatever contortion had pleased the populace then, I wished it might work its mojo now. "What's got them so pumped up? Is it the scare with Spinks?"

"Better," Cray said. "Levis is dead."

"Wow! Why are they so riled?"

I saw a malicious twinkle in his eyes. "Do you know what a hecatomb is, Eddie?"

"Human sacrifice?"

"The people of Dig City demand it. They get this way every time there's a bit of excitement around here." Cray shoved me out beneath the tunnel ceiling's proscenium, where big toe, an attention-galvanizing gavel, bumped thumpily against an antique newspaper vending machine, the makeshift podium. For a second all was silent except for Cray snickering in the wings. In the conniving ivories of his devilish grin, I could see he was primping himself for the role of begrudging Brutus in the prevailing putsch. I squeezed my eyes shut in an effete attempt to make it go away, then a mad cacophony welled up in the hall. For an ostrich's instant, I thought what I heard was applause, but looking I saw the motionless mass, the thousand blank expressions. The thunder above was just a train going by on the Red Line, constructed in 1917 and known as "the Rattler" for better than a century.

Psychologists say politicians never got enough affection during infancy and spend the rest of their lives over-compensating, trying to make literally everyone love them. If that was the case, then I supposed I had it coming when I set myself up for this moment. It had taken me a shrimp boat of hubris spilling over to get here: the hushed hall, the grotesque ocean of eyes cresting before me in a tsunami of indignation. Why had I not just enjoyed the life of the educated grifter and remained in the Nec with Shep? Or, after discovering the unseemly patrimony, why had I not simply accepted the congenital imperative and adapted to the comfortable ways of a Corrente? Why had I gotten sidetracked from the honest work of a hackney operator, with nobody to bother and no one to be bothered by except the hundred-odd passengers haranguing me every day? The answer was elementary enough:

so that I could make it down here for a public disemboweling at the hands of a dour, disenfranchised counterculture. I was not even a puppet, unless you're thinking along the lines of Punch and Judy. I was more like a piñata. They were propping me up for a pillory!

As long as I was not going to get out of there alive, I decided I might as well cast my lot in favor of a challenge to their revolutionary principles. I could at least use the opportunity to prod them a little on their pretensions of thrift. I figured, what did I have to lose, and decided to let loose. My brief flirtation with Jocy had convinced me they were capable of greater than that which lame Levis had laid out for them. I cleared my throat loudly, dankly, with all the charm and music of a finger bowl full of wet walnuts, and spoke. "As I understand it, these ceremonies are not about popularity, so I'm going to tell it like it is. The overworld upper class has been hoarding its stores long enough."

I thought I detected a restless, harping hiss amplifying in the audience. Or was it just steam from the sewers?

"It's the earth's winds, rivers, and fossil fuels that provide the current which three centuries ago Benjamin Franklin, the great revolutionary, first harvested."

There went up a murmur I took to be the murderous disapproval of the mass. Like Socrates willingly sipping his hemlock, I was satisfied to imbibe their indignation—the measure! Executed at Athens, that brainy ancient, who has been described as he-who-did-not-write, had likely held in mind's eye a lovely morsel—its beauty the material analogy of truth—of stripling Alcibiades; so I, delivering my unapologetic apologia, did envision a no-less-comely hunk of my fair beloved, Jocy.

"These are trying times. Just when an enemy has been defeated, you discover your leader has fallen. Whomever you choose as your next chief, Dig City, may he or she, by whatever peaceful means, provide the people with their share of power."

When they surged toward me like an army of zombies, I could not make out the message of their menacing incantation. I saw the tide rolling toward me, grabbing hands reaching greedily for my sleeves, cuffs, and collar, and I knew that huffing around the subterranean dead ends like a maze-trapped rat would just waste everyone's precious oxygen. I shut my eyes, swelled my chest, and breathlessly awaited the drawing and quartering, the undefiled image of Jocy's ass in my imagination a talisman of booming truth, the brimming scales of justice, the American way I could never escape, amen! But instead of being torn apart in the Comb, I was lifted up, hoisted atop shoulders, and showered with salutatory spanks.

Not only did the citizens of Dig City want me to stay, they wanted me to run the place, no questions asked. No family history to discourage me, no home to go to: With a little reluctance, I allowed them to crown me a cardboard Caesar.

My first order of business was to get a briefing on the state of the state from my Minister of Information. Besides being Dig City's self-designated seer, Terry was also the mastermind behind infrastructure. He sat at his touch term and told me all about the way things work. Animated diagrams projected on the walls of the Hive dramatized his demo.

Dig City was virtually impregnable. To keep the 1950s highway open during construction, workers hollowing out the tunnels at the end of century 20 had reinforced ceilings and walls with strong slurry. Floor pilings were sunk forty feet into bedrock, so the bottom would not drop out from under us any time soon. America's first subway made an awful racket at spots, but thousands of tons of good Baltimore steel would never relent. Dig City maintained control of the vent buildings and pump houses, which kept air in and water out. The thermal processes of the earth, along with a few propitious natural gas deposits, supplied enough heat to keep DC at a temperate, if clammy, sixty-five degrees. Gardens thrived under grow lights in the humid southern tunnels beneath Milk Street Atomic, the Beast's nuclear power plant. Organic fertilizers, artificial light, and step techniques applied to the nitrogen-rich soils yielded surplus harvests. Anything lacking in the mundis sub rosa could be obtained by a few overworld sympathizers who helped camouflage our elaborate system of ventilation, suction, and induction.

"What about the harbor and the closeness of the ocean?"

"The tide varies by nine feet every six hours and twenty-five minutes," Terry said, "but Dig City is waterproof to between five and ten feet below the floor, plus our pumps are in great shape. Every section of substructure is held down by gravity slabs and further anchored with tie rods. Thanks to Cape Cod, the continental shelf is actually more than a hundred miles from here, so there's enough sweet water in the table to last a thousand years, even without the rainwater reservoirs upstairs."

"Any chance the Beast might try to sabotage life support?"

"When it comes to basic resources, we would be able to hold out longer on everything—everything, that is, but one thing."

"What's that?"

"Air. A protracted outage that depletes our backup generators could leave us without adequate oxygen."

"Shouldn't we get some of our engineers working on ventilation alternatives?"

"We have a mole upstairs who goes by the codename

Hermanito. He's analyzed the ventilation situation, and the reports suggest it's not a cause for concern. Dig City and the Beast are symbiotic organisms. If overworld ever tried to shut us down, they would experience the same power privations. As long as their electrical plants are running, we'll have our air. Besides, we're all beholden to the same boss, and Hermanito says he's a sympathizer."

"Who's that?"

"Apple Jack, the new mayor."

You can bet I bit my lip at that nugget of Dig City politics. Now I knew it would be especially necessary for me to protect my identity. In my estimation, Apple Jack was one to keep a promise, and if he ever found out about who had just been elevated to DC's highest office, it would mean the end of not only this hustler's regal weekend, but maybe even the whole underground colony.

"When do I get to meet this Hermanito?"

"Sorry, Eddie." Terry said. "Hermanito is the cornerstone of Dig City intelligence. I can't risk blowing his cover."

On the spot, I thought: If anyone went snooping around Spinks's den, they might make the connection to the accident in the Ted Williams tunnel and maybe trace me all the way back to Pauly and Apple Jack.

"In order to forestall future sabotage," I suggested, "we should seal off Pan-Harbor Command."

"Sure," said Terry.

So goes my first decree.

In one of the air shafts onto Chinatown, a wall had been knocked out into the cellar of an out-of-business Asian grocery to create the commander's quarters, known as the Nest. Terry assured me this was one of the safest spots in Dig City. As it did not belong to the regular network of tunnels and shafts that made up the former artery, overworld authorities were not aware of its existence. I went back to my new cell to lie down, take inventory, maybe snatch a nap. My narrow bed sat on the pronounced incline of an out-of-service loading belt, directly beneath bulkhead doors that swayed onto Kneeland Street sidewalk.

The camaraderie around Dig City reminded me of that around the Nec, which, although aboveground, had been similarly cell-like: someone's breathing always a few inches from mine; the sense of ambitious projects, however pie-in-the-sky, to occupy our time; and the energy—ever-replenishing, seemingly inexhaustible—of us-against-them. After giving up my life as a road rat, it had been this tight-knittedness I had missed most, but there was something different this time. I had slept soundly back with the rats, but in the Hive I'd been given a poisonous gift, the sweetest nectar of duress: I lay awake contemplating a voluptuous figure. Overnight I needed somebody, and it did not matter whether a reawakened impulse toward altruism was polluted by this new-found acquisitiveness, for, just as surely as I would have to awaken to the electrically illuminated day and let my lungs breathe the artificially-circulated air, I would need to allow each to evolve unencumbered; my every exhalation seemed to sound her name: Jocy!

Before I could doze, Cray burst into my cell with his next big surprise. "The wedding is in half an hour."

"Who's getting married?"

"You and Jocy."

All the colony came out to the Comb. It was a simple, civil ceremony. I had a hard time keeping my eyes off Jocy's big butt in her bell-bottoms. Although Dig City thrift would have us eschew the extravagance of a reception, Jocy and I stood forever in the receiving line, where I met our fair-skinned subjects one-by-one. Mitts swollen from all the glad-handing, I walked Jocy back to her cell. Besides the vows, this was our first opportunity to speak since the night of my arrival. I stood by her door, rigid as a cigar-store Indian.

"I'm sorry," I stammered, "to hear about the chief."

"Don't you get it, Eddie? You're in charge now."

"Sure, but what about Levis of late?"

"Nobody is too shaken up by the loss. He wasn't doing the community any good. It would be better if you just forget about him." Gently, Jocy touched my hand. "Goodnight, Eddie. See you tomorrow in the Hive."

I sure had come a long way since the days doing partridge pose and picking pockets in the Beast. Eddie King: I was not completely certain I wanted the new job, but I was psyched it came with a queen. Cray had told me that the marriage was purely for PR, but still I was ascendant: Who was to say she would not eventually come to love me? I wondered what the mourning period was down here. What would merit the level of my infatuation? Would I wait a year? Five? Ten? Fifteen for the queen? None of those figures seemed prohibitive, nor did I register a blip of reluctance. Already, in my monotonous young life, I had become used to paying dues. And man! would she be worth it!

The clomping of commuters just inches above my head began at 5:30 AM—talk about incentive to get a jump on the day! As it was, the job I had set for myself would require medical-intern hours. I began implementing a plan to bring about infrastructural autonomy. It had yet to be determined whether my dream was practical or just a wad in my pipe.

The overworld's resources had been underexploited for fear that Apple Jack would crack down on the occupation, but the Beast's infrastructural integration with the artery left light-lubbers no way to curtail how Dig City had been piggy-backing on their utilities. The parallel opposites shared the same gas, telecom, and electric. Where circuits were sparking, there was nothing wrong with connecting a few wires. It was like holding one's cup beneath an open tap. I was certain that Dig City could be making a lot more of its position if only we could leave behind bleeding-heart frugality and recognize that utilities were ours for the taking. Even the overlords would be better off for not hoarding their surplus if we just went ahead and took it. The slogan printed on posters plastered all over the tunnels: one nation, underground, with batteries and plug-juice for all.

Mornings, I read voraciously, surveying e-books on intentional communities of the last four hundred years, from Jamestown and Plymouth to Jonestown and Chunnelville. I admired J. H. Noyes and Oneida, although I was a little alarmed by the leader's enthusiasm for communal marriage. On the other hand, you had Father Rapp's Economy, a city of enforced celibacy. Legend had it he had accidentally killed his son while, in a rage over a broken rule, carrying out a hasty castration. I took the best stuff from these cults and added a dash of road rat's graft. Our workers hijacked truckloads of energy cells direct from factory lots and kept the juice flowing by continuous, systematic relocation of cryptic siphon grids that skimmed the upstairs neighbors everywhere from their city shafts to the transformers in corporate basements. Dig City's humble siphons were of course a minor nuisance to the utility companies and the businesses from whom we borrowed, but I was reminded of the pickpocket's creed: to steal, to purloin, and never to yield. It seemed like a wholesome ideology: clever utilization of an abundance that had been metered by an avaricious syndicate.

Terry and Cray were pretty tight-lipped about the details of what had happened to my predecessor, and delicacy proscribed my trying to pry the story out of Jocy, but legends of Levis's profligacy were popular currency. Levis had been an innovative architect, an able contractor, but ultimately no leader. After building the Dig City infrastructure, he began acting kooky. He took to going on boozing binges with his bodyguards. He would burst into song at state suppers. By the end, with his flamboyant couture and frequent personality lapses, Levis had been an embarrassment to the movement, and finally became estranged not just from his go-getter wife, but from the whole of the underground country. In the big scheme of things, Levis had done Dig City a favor by dropping out. His charisma had been convenient in the early days of the colony. He was the eccentric around whom the first Dig City immigrants had centered their discipline, but his heart had not really been with the revolution. According to some rumors, a compulsive gambling habit and reckless betting had embroiled him in dark debts. While trying to pay them off, Levis got wrought up in wild, cowboy histrionics. Out carousing on dangerous roads, some bandits had run him down—typical Mass highway robbery. Thus a luckless wayfarer ascended to his seat.

Ours became the wildest underground colony the world over, attracting thousands of immigrants, Afghan to Zulu. A whole new hybrid race emerged—or, rather, dug in deeper. The birth rate increased exponentially. Gambians got it on with Goans, Cubans taught Pakistanis how to mambo, and the kids kept coming. Of course, all those couplings brought their by-products, so I concentrated on improving the pediatrics program at Broodnest General, the underground hospital where our drop-out doctors made sure the little suckers arrived safely. With Dig City birthrate booming, the consuming domestic issue became education. I revamped the primary school system, drawing liberally on Shep's model. Every day, I appreciated a little more how the bogus blind man had prepared me, by his example, for my own stewardship of an orphan race.

Swift application of the promised policy won me fanatical support among editors of both the *Dig City Dirt* and the *Hole-in-the-Ground Herald*. Although the entire colony clearly appreciated the reforms and my popularity in subterranean polls soared, it was Jocy who always delivered the coup de grace that won the people's hearts. During one particularly pitched town meeting in the packed Comb, everybody in the parent–teacher association was arguing over the athletic program's mascot proposal. Most of the obvious underground icons were too easy and carried unflattering connotations: worms, moles, grubs, et cetera. I gamely suggested the Beetles, but Jocy bested me, all agreed, when she abbreviated the idea: the DC Bees. As symbol, the creature trafficked the very nectar of community, industriousness, and ingenuity, and the solution expedited the next item on the agenda (which, from other assemblies of the

PTA, I knew could drag on for hours of filibuster): school colors. Yellow and black stripes made for fantastic warm-up pants.

During my tenure, Dig City saw days of great growth and prosperity. Thanks to my administration's development of craft, light industry, underground agriculture and, of course, scavengery, the domestic product rose steadily. These were enchanted days. At first, nobody in the Beast batted an eyelash. Hermanito passed along intelligence that suggested Apple Jack and his staff were satisfied with the overworld byproducts of our colony: the homeless out of sight, a marked mitigation of urban blight. The denizens of Dig City were the white blood cells in the bypassed arteries of the city, our discrete circulation maintaining a glowing complexion on the surface. Over time, however, the aboveground powers began to take an unfavorable attitude toward our subterranean squat. We rankled by our example. Sixteenth Century and since, New England neighborhoods had been rendered socially homogeneous, with prejudice always a ready rallying cry to distract the working class and tolerance confined to tiny Rhode Island, the rest of the colonies' retarded cousin. By admitting anybody, regardless of race, ethnicity, religion, and sexual orientation, our underground occupation brought ineluctable integration, pushing the overworld's hand. After Dig City's example, marginalized groups above grade began to enhance efforts to band together. Synagogues and Baptist churches sponsored seder-barbecues and the Cambridge Gay Men's Choir won best float in the St. Patrick's Day parade. This sort of thing irritated the upstairs management, but I was too focused on public policy to pay attention to diplomacy.

Jocy had four children. It all happened so suddenly, it was

hard to believe they belonged to me. Being a father was kind of like being chief: a big fuss I felt like I had not merited but which had fallen into my lap. I could comprehend how playing a VR game had somehow won me the crown, but in all the excitement and overwork of running a shoestring mobocracy, I could not clearly recall copulation. There were so many all-nighters at the Hive, punctuated by my return, wrecked, to the Nest, that the jobs might have happened anywhere in there, even in my sleep. I was a little irked that I could not remember the presumably passionate nights that had yielded two sons and two daughters, but the term in my cell accessed some of the hottest bottom sites on the Net, and I copped frequent quickies and pulled occasional all-nighters with good ol' Mrs. Palmer, man's other best friend, who lives at the end of Arm Street. Lending new pertinence to my private appreciation of the nickname Fast Eddie, I sublimated all the energies of pseudo-celibacy into that most favored game of solitaire. Personal space was of course hard to come by in Dig City, but early on I settled on a special place as my private getaway. Adjacent to the Hive there was a classical lavatory, three stalls and a sink left over from the days when the Beast had staffed this section of the Central Artery/Tunnel. Terry and Cray understood I got my best thinking done on the throne. "Eddie's off to write a letter to Apple Jack," they joked. I preferred the center stool. Here, I conceived projects, hammered out plans, and worked through problems between brief flights of onanistic bliss. It cleared my mind, gave me a kick, and I got it over with quickly. Other executives have been just as effective while occasionally indulging in a little slapple and tic.

One Sunday, gray and rainy, I awoke in the Nest with a

start and an erection. The same clues as ever told me about the weather up there: the rivulets seeping through the cracks and along the foot of the wall, provocative droplets condensing pregnantly on the metal portal above my bed. Best of all was an aspect I could not recall experiencing since I had accidentally descended into this deleterious scene, likely as not because a constellation of circumstances had not yet conspired to keep me here in bed on one of the sixty-or-so days of the year that commercial traffic was not thundering overhead: The inch or so of steel that separated my compact domicile from the well-trodden sidewalk was beset by the mystical patter of precipitation. When had Jocy and I last done it? I seemed to recall suckling a breast, but it felt like a far-off, remote notion. Could it have been before our honeymoon? When had I ever, I groggily contemplated, enjoyed congress with the lady who made an us out of me, in lucid morning vitality, on that day engineered for such enjoyment, under romantic summer rain's trill and timpani? If ever, I could not remember.

My hand was idly following such thoughts when someone burst into the Nest. I was scrambling to cover up when I saw it was Terry. "Cray has called an emergency cabinet meeting, Eddie."

"What is it?"

"Hermanito up above has been sending us some alarming messages. Apple Jack's getting ornery."

I hurried to the Hive, worried that the emergency might have something to do with me. Jocy was waiting. Cray looked grave. "The mayor's got an old score to settle," he said.

"What's the grudge?" I held my breath, ruminating: I knew it! Apple Jack finally figured out it's Eddie Corrente at the helm here. Still holding a grudge from when I was caught trespassing at Adelle's, he's now issuing a deadly summons.

"It's about the death of Levis, his old friend. AJ's convinced that whoever killed him is hiding out down here."

Briefly relieved, I breathed. "I don't get it. From what I'm told, nobody liked Levis anyway."

Jocy said, "Everybody hates Apple Jack, too. Maybe that's why he and Levis got along."

"Any idea what Apple Jack might do?"

"I bet it won't take us long to find out," Terry said. "Our only choice is to re-open the Levis investigation."

Terry and Cray went off to contact Hermanito, leaving Jocy and me alone in the Hive. "This is ridiculous," Jocy said. "Everyone knows Levis was killed by thieves at the Crossroads . . . . What's wrong, Eddie? You look ruddy."

"Strange, hearing you just now . . . my mind wandered, my thoughts racing back and forth."

"What do you mean? Why so anxious?"

"I thought I heard you say that Levis was cut down at the Crossroads."

"That was the story. It hasn't died out yet."

"Where did this thing happen? Be precise."

"The Crossroads tavern under the casino in East Beast— at least, that's the last place Levis was seen alive before he got hammered in the Ted Williams tunnel."

"When? How long ago?"

"The *Herald* no sooner reported Levis dead then you appeared and they hailed you King of the Bees." I buckled over at a sudden cramp. "Eddie, are you okay?"

"I think I'm coming down with something."

I went next door to the lavatory to work this one through. The weird coincidence about Levis's death was a minor mind-blower, but I reminded myself that the TW was a highway-man's favorite spot for the quick crash and dash. There was a new accident in there every week. Still, the little detail about the timing was messing with more than just my head.

It wasn't so funny anymore, that joke about writing AJ a letter. Constipated, I couldn't move. It must have been the pressure getting to me. I needed refreshed perspective, and so chose to invoke a long-lost obsession. I recalled my fondness for an old premise: Pretend Pauly Corrente's dead.

I pictured Merry at the wake, buxom in black mini-dress, pillbox hat cocked just so, eyes peeking coyly from under beaded mesh, seeming less like grieving Penelope than wily Scheherazade. In my mind, her bosom heaving, daubing opulent tears with a kerchief, Merry has not aged, only ripened. A hundred sudden suitors, from assistant traffic engineers to county selectmen, each scheming to be her comforter, mill around the ground floor of our house. Did I say "our"? Yes, I suppose I feel a little possessive. I walk in, a passion of protectiveness welling in my breast, and reclaim my home, vanquishing the stewards of the status quo. In a second, Merry is towing me through the house, weaving between charcoal suits. "We have to be alone." In the study, she sidles onto Pauly's commode and sits me on her lap. A proud son, I bask in Merry's bountiful embrace and tell her all about how far I've come from the kid she worried would never get his nose out of the arcade: the rescue of Dig City (she is pleased to know I have become a politician just like Pauly), the lovely wife (the kind any boy's mother would be proud to have brought home to her), the chance children—stripling girls, strapping boys.

All of a sudden our reunion was ruptured. Merry's veil was rended with a dreadful sibilance and the Corrente study melted away. I sat alone on a throne in Dig City with an insufferable stench and something else, a sensation I could not place. There was that noise again, like a great tearing of cloth— somebody occupied the stall to the right of mine. Cray and Terry were doing detective work and there was no way my immaculate Jocy could be giving birth to such dischord. Had one of the guards gotten dyspepsia?

A man called over his own cacophonous racket, "'Little help—any TP over there?" Had my noxious neighbor detected the tempo of my self-gratification? My ears burning with embarrassment, I reached for the roll. Filled with a terrible foreboding, I experienced a synesthetic short-circuit provoked by a stimulus foreign yet familiar, something which, as airborne, could have been visible, audible, olfactory, palpable, palatable: furtive whispers? green felt blotters? sour lemon? I could not name the nature of the offending atoms in the air, but presently, in the flicker of reflex it took me to toss the tube at a pair of shabby shoes that weren't DC issue, it came to mind as a word, a neologism, albeit rather retro for neo, speaking itself at last as a bit of blather that, even over the stink, could have been referenced by any one of the senses: Pep-O-mint.

I bent over and peeped under the partition. It was Metzger, the orphan broker, screwed-up features, jaundice, and all. "Eddie King, huh?"

"What are you doing here?"

Metzger strained at his task, his face puckered in that acrid expression I remembered from our first meeting. "What does it look like I'm doing?" he said, punctuating derision with a dissonant sizzle.

"I mean how did you find me?"

"Nobody in the shepherding business ever loses track of a contact." After another toot, Metzger piped down and managed a crooked grin. "I've got good news, Eddie. Pauly Corrente is dead."

At that instant, the bathroom bulb burned out, blotting the room with a clap of darkness. A shudder passed through me. Could my fantasy have come true? It was as if by my musing I had summoned the news. "What happened?" I called out in the gloom.

"A light tip of scales put the old bones to rest," Metzger said. "Pauly was going at it in the sack. That Jersey jerk left you half his estate. I figure you give me a third and we're even. Plus there's one more shepherd who gets a cut."

I breathed a sigh of relief into the midst of the fragrant eclipse. The two-time mayor of America's most congenial city had perished of causes not entirely unnatural, if abetted by over-exertion. The burden had been lifted from my conscience. There was no way I could hurt Pauly now, either by my reckless mishap with Apple Jack or by any other means.

Metzger was gassing on: "With the sensation you'll cause by your return, it's not too late to get in the mayor's race. A person can make a lot of lucrative deals as a suburban politician, and you're a shoe-in for the office, Eddie. As soon as we're done in here we'll get going to Ho-Ho-Kus?"

A bubble of indigestion caused me to bend double. "Are you kidding? There's no way I can go back there."

"What are you talking about? Most grifters would kill for this gig. Corrente lived like a king!"

The arrogant, flatulent parasite was aggravating my colic, and the fact that I couldn't see him and show him I was angry got me even more worked up. "Pauly was a plumber. He made his billions in shit."

"Now he's buried in the garden state with the rest of the radioactive waste."

"And then there's Merry—I swear she was hitting on me."

"So? You should shtup her! Merry's part of the deal: the cherry atop the torte. . ."

"You're talking about my mother, fucker!"

". . . No dog, that's for sure . . ."

"She happens to be the one I'm a son of, bitch."

". . . There's probably a lot of ride left in that mare . . ."

"The lineage responsible for my long mules, jackass."

". . . Nice tits!"

"Quit it!"

Metzger grunted, let one rip. "So this female phobia of yours made you run from the Correntes?"

"And my *dad*, old man—so I wouldn't kill my dad. Duh."

"You're fooling yourself, Eddie. Pauly wasn't your pa."

"What do you mean?"

"Let me tell you something about the brotherhood of herdsmen: We don't meddle with each other's indentures without permission. I was going to pocket your front money way back when, but an old friend, the shepherd I was talking about, gave me the okay to place you. You were so dead-set on finding out where you come from I figured I might as well make it some nice, fancy folks. Your timing was lucky; the Correntes were on the market."

In the midst of all the wind, I had to be sure I had heard him correctly. I spelled it out in the funky void: "Pauly's not my father and Merry's not my mother?"

"No way. The mayor had some kind of problem with sperm count. Merry was never once pregnant. You have about as much match to Corrente DNA as me, Eddie."

Metzger could not have given me a better present. Boom! I was a bastard again.

The door to my stall blasted open and a sudden spotlight burned my eyes. "Man! it stinks in here!" Cray said.

I squeezed my knees together and ducked the flashlight beam. Under the partition, I saw the toilet paper nestled at the foot of the bowl next-door, but the shoes were gone. Metzger wasn't there. Whoa! I thought to myself, I must have been hallucinating. I had conjured a chimera. Pauly's necrology and the rest of the conversation had been a dream within a dream, no more real than my daydream with Merry, but I had been unable to distinguish the fallacy. My fantasies were getting the better of me. This was what happened when a person with my luck dug up such submerged sludge.

"It's a hostile outage, Eddie," Cray said. "We're not getting secondary power sources from anywhere on the grid."

"Come on, Cray," I said, shading my eyes. "There have always been flashes and flickers." I crossed my legs and held a little bouquet of tissue at my lap.

"This one is different. The mayor, in cahoots with the city council and the overlords of private utilities, called for a Sunday shut-off across selected sectors. That dirtbag Apple Jack cut off electrical service to the entire area above Dig City. Darkness, uninterrupted, consumes every tunnel."

"But doesn't this knock them out upstairs, too?"

"They're ready to suck it up to flush us out from down under. Apple Jack knows we'll run out of oxygen, and he has already announced that he anticipates a complete evacuation within twenty-four hours. Air. They've got us there."

"But I thought we had temporary alternatives. Isn't there anything we can finesse to get out of this mess?"

"Even with the backup generators, the clean air supply won't last through the night. Within a few hours, toxicity will reach problem levels. By afternoon, every citizen will be subject to side effects like those of altitude sickness: nausea, dizziness, delirium. The end result could be asphyxiation." Cray aimed the flashlight at my eyes. "What are you doing in here, anyway, Eddie?"

Squinting up into the beam, I said, "Uh, not feeling so hot."

"Make it fast," he said, shutting the stall door. "I've got to go rev up the generators." Cray left the lavatory.

I should have seen it coming. The inception of his third term had given birth to the temperamental monarch in Apple Jack, and now our underground occupation was his first target. There had not been this kind of emergency since Miss Spinks had pulled that prank slamming the tunnel doors shut. If I did not come up with a solution expeditiously, it would mean the end of Dig City. But I was stuck. All I had been able to manage with my Merry fantasy was triggering a weird relapse. How had I let myself get so desperate? Then again, I had never been entirely stable. All along, those pathological impulses had just been suppressed. Now, with a crisis at hand, I was back to borderline, and frequent erotic exercise had left my imagination overdeveloped. Funny, I could swear I still sensed the Pep-O-mint.

When the generators kicked in, supplying just enough juice to put the bulbs at tepid yellow, I felt a little better. Now maybe I would be able to get things moving. But the reprieve was short-lived. I heard an inquisitive sniff, this time to the left.

Another familiar voice, different from that of the phantom patrimony peddler: "Who is that? I smell a rat."

"It's me: Eddie," I said, trembling.

"Baby Eddie? Eddie Feet? Fast Eddie? Eddie Pussy?"

I bent over to sneak a peek. There he was, upside-down in dark glasses, handicapped act, and the same old stained shirt. Fuses blowing in the murky light, I cried, "How did you get here?"

Grinning like the dickens, Shep said, "I was about to ask you the same thing. This is definitely a demotion from the Nec. What have they got you on? Sewer duty?"

In a flash I reverted to virulent rat. "I happen to have a management position—more than you were ever able to offer."

"You abandoned me, Eddie. Wasn't I was your friend? Didn't I look out for you? Didn't I treat you like a son?"

"You shouted at me. You made me hustle change. You stole my food."

"See? I was like a father to you!"

I refused to believe my eyes. Maybe oxygen deprivation was affecting my senses. I put my head between my knees and took a couple of quick deep breaths. This was turning into a twisted *Christmas Carol*. "Shep, if it's really you, tell me this: Who was my mother—?"

"What's the use in wondering, Eddie? Mother is an empathic computer on the spaceship of the soul who learns how to think and goes berserk . . . Mother is a tea-sipping, non-chalant, male manager for an underground cortege of agents named X . . . Mother is the mummified remains belonging to a madman's once-mother, stacked skeletally in a rocking chair at a broken-down motel . . ."

I craned my head under the partition and shouted, "All right, already! Shut up!"

Shep made that lock-the-mouth-and-throw-away-the-key gesture from days of petty, juvenile secrets, sitting with arms crossed and a pursed-lipped expression that, under the circumstances, pantomimed by a pretend-sightless man, struck me as doubly enraging. From the other stall came a thunderous crack. I craned around to the right. Metzger was back.

"Where'd you go?"

"Actually, I never left." He bent his legs demonstratively. Not one to risk getting stung, Metzger had put his feet up on the seat.

"Is this the one you meant," I said, with a thumb back toward Shep, "the other shepherd who handed me off to you?"

Metzger said, "He's your man."

"Shep, you know this guy?"

"Can't say I don't recognize the voice," Shep said. "I gave Metzger the okay to take you, Eddie. That's standard practice with a pack master's property."

Metzger said. "Ditch Dig City, Eddie. This place is going down the tubes."

I sucked in my gut, snapped up, and snapped out of it. "You two are just polluting precious air." I bailed out of my stall, retaining a painful plug. Pausing at the sink, I said, "I'm going to get the guards. They'll take you both back where you came from." In the mirror, I saw their doors swing open.

"Oh, sure!" Metzger said. "You just want Corrente's inheritance all to yourself. Be reasonable, Eddie. You're not going to forget the old fellows who made you a fortune, are you?"

Flicking water droplets from my fingertips, I turned to face the squatting grouches. "What if I let you split all the money?"

Shep didn't miss a beat. "Sounds pretty fair."

"Tell me something first. Where did I come from?"

"Beats me," Metzger said. "I never bothered to check."

Shep gnawed his lower lip.

"Hoard the secret any longer," I said, "and the big payoff goes down the drain."

"Go ahead and tell him," Metzger said. "What harm could it do?"

"Okay, Eddie," my old patron said. "You asked for it."

I didn't have any time to waste, but I was so surprised to see Shep concede that I sat up on the edge of the sink.

"A long time ago, before I opened the Nec, I used to run with a wild crowd. There was this friend of mine who played poker. He was always burning up and down the interstates after the high stakes. I'd go along sometimes on rides, hang around during the game. Everyone believed I was really blind—see the potential advantage? Anyway, my buddy liked to play with fire. His favorite was five-card stud, jokers wild, and this one time he challenged Apple Jack to a match. I don't have to tell you that idea was bad. You know how these things go: Final round, he had already put everything he had on the table, but they both had one more card coming, so by the showdown Apple

Jack proposed a blind bet. They wrote down what they wanted from each other on two slips of paper and put them in the pot. Guess what Apple Jack asked for?"

"His life? His wife?"

"Close. Just to fuck him over, Apple Jack had written: *your motherfucking firstborn.*"

"You're telling me I was bet away in a poker game?"

"Rash tactics, but your dad had a great hand. For a couple of scoundrels, he and Apple Jack had been pretty good friends, although what happened at the call changed that fast. Apple Jack showed ten-to-king, all spades, while your dad showed a joker and three bullets—"

"Bullets?"

"Bullets, pocket rockets—aces, Eddie. It looked like Apple Jack might have gotten the mortal nuts, a royal flush, but your father believed he had the nutcracker. When it came time to roll, he thought he had snagged the pot. You know what beats a straight flush? Five of a kind. It doesn't have to be aces, but in your daddy's case it was, which was bad news for baby. When they turned over their hole cards is when he lost more than just the game: Apple Jack shows a flush, ace high, your father's got a joker and four aces—it doesn't add up. There was one too many spadey Ays, which isn't cool with honest AJ. He can't stand getting stuck, and it enraged him to catch your dad trying to sneak lady luck out in her evening gown. Your father had plucked that second ace of spades from up his sleeve."

"But what could Apple Jack have wanted with a baby?"

"Nothing. He had just been joking, but the cheat routine made it a point of pride. In the end, the big boss did the noble thing by letting your father surrender the kid to me. That's what happened the day you of the flappy feet ended up the jester."

"What about my mother?"

"Your father snuck you out of the crib while she was asleep. Oh, the old lady was pissed, but you can't fight Apple Jack."

"Where did this all go down? Southie? Sommerville?"

"Down here, Eddie. Dig City. Your mom is still a big figure in the movement."

"How big?"

"For one thing, she's got a booming booty."

Gulp. "You mean . . . a large behind?"

"The mud-flap kind. Big feet, too, but she always wears bell-bottoms to cover them up."

I was at the edge of hearing horrors, but I had to hear. "And my father?"

"Crazy cat, built this place, drove a rig."

A sinister quiver passed through me. *That big eight-wheeler runnin' down the track means your true lovin' daddy ain't a-comin' back.* "A trucker? What was his handle?"

"He called himself the King."

Double whammy! Daddy had been Levis, the King, and I had summoned him to a deadly collision that day at the Crossroads. Jocy was mother and I had done her. Raving, I thrashed and raged. The glasses got torn off my face in the melee. Either Shep or Metzger stepped on them: I heard the lenses shatter.

Crowds stomped overhead and I cowered, covering my ears against the reports reverberating through the metal doors, shutting my eyes to the sight of the loading-belt bed where I lay, the location of who knows how many incestuous copulations. I clutched my stomach, bent double and ready to barf like I had swallowed a good gob of tobacco juice. Apple Jack's *motherfucker* echoed in my head together with Adelle's fortune: *PS: He lives*—and dad had, back then, but I had iced him in the TW tunnel. In the interval, I had married mom: All along, the crystal springs of blissful ignorance had been polluted by the murky waters of my leader-libido. If I had been given a little more information, I might have figured it out for myself, but I had been groping blindly in the dark.

"Eddie, it's me, Shep," my old master said, kneeling beside me in the dim Nest. Without glasses, I was blind as a baby whose eyelids have not parted. "You must have picked up a wicked parasite. Hang in there; Metzger's got a plan to get you up and out of here."

"Just let me lie here for a little while, I'll be fine," I moaned, but I knew I was that which had to be regurgitated, the toxin at the heart of Dig City's pollution. There was no way the underground could hold me down. If I went ahead and sacrificed myself to the overworld, just as Levis had done to the infant-me, maybe Apple Jack would lift the plague of bad air. I wanted to be gone before anyone—uncle-brother-in-law Cray, mother-wife Jocy, or my melodramatic sibling-children—could see me.

Shep heaved the portal open and pushed me up to the level of the street, slamming the door behind me. The assault of light was a cosmic club on the head, Zeus clobbering me with his shoe. Sun! I wept, and it was for much more than irritation of my long-dilated pupils. In the ultimate indignity since having been dubbed Eddie Feet, I was exiled from the Hive. Some heavy headgear, a cumbersome construction of plaster and wire mesh, was thrown over my shoulders, pinning my arms to my side. Suddenly snared, I awakened to reality. A few inches from my pupils, everything was fuzzy through a narrow slit bordered by a nest of feathers and a shimmering canopy of sequins, but I could tell that the early morning shower had passed and now Chinatown was choked with festival-goers. So abruptly yoked, I didn't have time to get my bearings when a punt at my can accompanied Metzger's hissed command, "Dance."

I had no choice. The shepherd took his job seriously enough so that if I did not step to, I knew, I would suffer another poke. I did the funky chicken, feebly protesting, "I can't see!"

"We're a dragon, all right? Now keep moving."

Amid continuous reports, we high-stepped across a carpet of firecracker paper. I found myself nose to nose with the owner of one of the ubiquitous groceries. He held out a thousand-dollar bill, placing it almost all the way in the crepe-paper mouth, and I snatched reflexly at his idle holiday offering. The dull electrical thrum of a long-slumbering thrill shook right out of the ground, up my leg, and into my spine. I might have forgotten my disgrace and gone over the whole route to pocket a great day's take, but another well-parlayed pestle at the heart of my mortar told me it was time to bob and weave away.

Wheeled around by a switch of dark genius in the nether end of the monster we pretended to be, I found myself standing face-to-fire-breathing-tongue with my blurry enemy. Huffing down on me: Mayor Apple Jack, breath fetid as ever, Chinese donut crumbs stuck to his cinder block chin. My heart beat uproariously enough, it would seem, to betray me despite the din, and the blood in my ears burned as hot as the boiling shot of soup inside those innocent looking Asian dumplings. Hizzoner, goldly guffawing, was looking past me, evidently mugging for some kind of pict op, and, I recognized almost too late, trying to shove something down my papier-mâché throat. It was one of those cheap keys mayors foist on suckers at public functions. "Are you going to swallow this chunk of brass," he growled into a glass eye set a foot above my actual head, "or do I climb in and shove it up your ass?" I accepted the token with a gulp! and my tail and I were on the run.

At the edge of the festival, Metzger lifted the costume off and, brandishing cuffs, grabbed my hands. I held out the G-note and the key to the city. When Metzger grabbed, I bolted, leaving him holding the bait and shackled.

Stooped, clutching my stomach, I pushed my way through the throng and under the great, oriental gate to the accompaniment of gong dong and cymbal crash. My irises adjusted to the light, but without glasses I could focus no definite shapes beyond my palm, and not even that with my arm outstretched. Everyone I bumped into punctuated their watch-where-you're-goings with grumbled *motherfuckers*. To weak eyes, the Mandarin signs all seemed to read *patricide*. All the same, I knew where I had to go. I was like the sick man rushing to the toilet to throw up, only it was me, everything I represented, that I needed to flush. I felt nauseous and cold. I couldn't shut off an audio loop playing over and over in my skull, a sample out of a juke box tune from the days of Apple Jack's Paramus arcade. Atonal organ, ruminative guitar, free-form percussion, gritty baritone: "Father?" "Yes, son." "I want to kill you . . . Mother? I want to—" The growl turned into a howl.

I must have looked like a madman staggering to the end of Long Wharf under the skeleton of the bombed-out Marriott. It wasn't exasperation—or any other dramatic aspect of how we might expect madness to take shape—that led me to the edge of the dock. It was more like indifference. I had almost died a dozen times, not a few of them by my own hand. During particularly dark chapters, a latent fascination with suicide had been the only thing that had kept me from killing myself. The fetish for one's own death is great incentive to stay alive. The promise of another day brooding on the exigency of the end depends, after all, on survival. Now there was nothing keeping me from finishing the job. Light! let me look my last on you. Not to be born is best. Call no man fortunate that is not dead. Disgraced by exposure of my execrable incest, I felt around in the heap of jetsam for plumb and tackle. Cast off at the end of the crumbling pier, I found some braided rope and a weight of the nautical variety used to keep lobster traps from getting dragged away by currents: iron, with an iron loop at one end to receive the line from rigging or cage. Letting both feet dangle over the water, I tied one end of the rope to the anchor, the other around my feet, and, like a paramedic marking the ETD, cast a last glance at the watch on my wrist.

In the shadow of black pillars, by the crumbling compass mosaic, the day was dimming with the overtones of a deepening bruise. Just as the sky's light would diffuse into the leaden sea, so the darkening medium seemed ready to accept me. After all, gravity had stuck me to earth all my life. Wouldn't it now, at the edge of the world, drag me into a bold, new element? Who cared about what dreams may come? I was ready for them, so long as they would cease the steady irrelevance: the senseless conflicts that had jettisoned me to this remote outpost of barbarian territory, the meaningless momentum that had dragged the neo-savages to New England in the first place. Long had I lived a subterranean life. Now, at the edge of this cold continent, where swamp meets ocean, I would graduate to an eternity submarine. Compared to open sea, the harbor was just a shallow tub, but enough to ship this struggling knot of nerves once and for all. It only takes a teaspoon. Great, gaping bay!—mouth onto the awesome, insatiable Atlantic—you take all the earth feeds you. What has not been deposited at your lips by land's overspilling ladle?

I was ready to take the final dive when out of nowhere came a sultry slur: "If you're looking for trouble, you came to the right place."

Once again, I recognized the voice—the twang rang like an alarm in my head. He was right behind me. The outline was fuzzy, but it sure looked like leather. "Is it really you?"

"Who am I," he vamped, "that the King would bleed and die for?"

It was Levis, the King, my dad. *PS: He lives* came back to me again, this time in the creepy sense of resurrection. Was it a father's shade come to greet his son at the border of Hades? "I must be dead," I said.

Levis leaned so close I could smell the sarcasm, enough to sink a small island-state: "Only the strong survive."

The stink of that cynical grin brought me back to my senses. How could I have been so naïve? I knew this trick: the reverse–Trojan horse! If you say there's nothing up your sleeve, people become suspicious; but they lap it up when you show them an empty vessel and say you've made something disappear. "You weren't even in the TW that day," I blubbered. "You just burned the high beams and sent that truck down the tunnel with a brick on the accelerator."

"Play it, son!"

Levis's dump truck had been such a convincing hat, I had failed to notice there was never a rabbit. "You just wanted to play dead."

"I got my mojo working, but it just don't work on you."

"You set me up to take a dive! Your own child!"

Levis lowered his dark shades. "But that's the best part, Eddie. You're not. Jocy never let me in her cell when the wedding was done. She had somebody's son, but it wasn't mine. You're just a joker, wild. You're an ace from another pack."

Disease and dementia departed; the poles in my lobes were reversed. The day was still out of focus, but the metropolis sang a hosanna: the ingenious brainstorming of jackhammers! the roar of muscle cars out on Northern Avenue! the patois of alarms getting tripped! "You mean. . . ?"

"You didn't kill me and I'm not your father."

I had caught my credulous cleft on treachery's hook, but now, half-acquitted, I tasted possibilities of release, of getting thrown back in the mystery, and, perhaps, of redemption. "When we met at the Crossroads, you weren't just fishing for any sucker to bump up against in the tunnel, were you?"

Levis shook a leg, did a little jig. "I gave you away as a baby and I thought the debt was paid, but as you grew, you kept scavenging for bits of history. When you had Metzger do those DNA tests, word got around that not only were you not my firstborn, you weren't mine at all. Trick Apple Jack once, you get a life indenture. Trick him twice, it's the death sentence. Rather than wait around for AJ to come get me, I decided to have a spectacular accident—and take you down for good measure. I never would have had to rig that crash if you hadn't kept scurrying around. You ratted on me, Eddie."

"You didn't even think about how Spinks had Dig City in the clink?"

"How about you? You've just left DC in some jam."

"All AJ wanted was your killer. Now that I'm up and out, he has to release the Bees."

"Wrong. Apple Jack was just riding your ass. The pressure's still on."

It dawned on me that I had to survive if Dig City, which Levis, in his deranged cynicism, had abandoned, was going to stand a chance at rescue. Shep never would have let me quit a trick like this, not without giving it the best flick of my wrist. It was a straitjacket escape I could not simply wrest my way out of alone: There was an entire colony strapped to my back. Why was I here, anyway, if not to protect these children orphaned by the earth? I was responsible as a father for every one of them, by an obligation greater than blood. A psychic contortion was required: I had to submerge the memory of that perverse maternal propinquity. Besides, Jocy, too, had been sorely deceived by Levis's scheme. However abominable our affiliation, I could not let it distract me from the next step. Yet without even the power to focus on this fugitive freak, I was still in a literal bind. This wasn't the first time he had tried to blow my mind. Inconspicuously working on the knot at my ankles, I endeavored to distract the maniac with questions. "Who was my real dad?"

"Ha!" he snorted. "When it comes to Jocy, who knows? She's so loose it could have been anybody. But I'll bet you one thing, whoever he was . . ." The shades went back in place. "They call your daddy Big Boots."

"Where have you been hiding out?"

"I've been traveling over mountains."

"And you never let on who you are?"

"Sometimes I feel like a motherless child," he replied. Again, Levis lowered his sunglasses. "But I knew I was sunk back when Apple Jack found out you weren't mine." He pulled something from his pocket. "This trinket came with my death warrant. AJ mentioned it belonged to you. Here, Eddie. I want you to have it back."

The sound of the *plink!* told me that Levis threw it in the drink.

"What'd you do that for?"

"So you can go after it." Levis kicked the weight over the edge of the dock and the line at my feet began rapidly unraveling. "No matter what you do, play it, son!"

I, a roped calf, was jerked injuriously against dock's edge, where rotting wood ripped into my rump. I went off the pier and into the frigid water of the harbor, fresh splinters stinging with brine. I kicked and thrashed, going down fast. A good, long rope had assured that the anchor would be well underway in its accelerated sinking by the time the tethered quarry followed. Now the plumb was plummeting, as it was designed to, in its vertical search for the nearest horizontal, which turned out to be pretty far from the liquid surface. The taste of blood rushing into my mouth commingling with the salt water invading gaping nostrils permeated my taste buds like a slice of tomato. Sound takes on a womb-like compression for creatures who bathe, as did I, in the embryonic fluid covering three-fourths of the globe. A small, coppery fin flitted and glimmered before my clouded eyes. I knew it could not be a goldfish, not in this dreck. It was the other item Levis had thrown in, and I clamped it between my teeth: One Cent!

The anchor sank into a foot of muck and the speed and chaos of plunge stopped. I was bound, stuck like a finger-sandwich toothpick in the excrement at the bottom of the bay, down among the beggar quahogs, down in the piles of rocks, bottles, and orphaned telephone lines, down where went beings unwanted and unmissed, down with me. This would require some hairy Houdini. Armies of contortionists, charmed and charlatan, have tried this escape, and not a few among the idiot arrivistes have succeeded, but for them it was a trick with predetermined parameters and an anticipated, if not rigged, departure. In my case the outcome involved a lobster.

She was about all I could see in front of me, bowing at my feet like a reluctant emissary in the inky sediment of the bleak, sun-deprived abyss. Call it dementia stemming from panic, but I understood, in the empathic language of these most highly organized crustaceans, what she was saying. I knew that she had come from Outer Harbor, not only because not even these legendary bottom feeders could stomach the mucky junk food down in Inner, but also since she was caught in a cage that trailed a severed line. I noted her gender for the copious combs of eggs clinging to the feathery hairs of her swimmerets. She could be carrying those for ten months, to term, if not for getting stuck in a stray starvation trap that had drifted in with the tide. Now no lobsterman would release her so that she could make a bigger harvest next year.

I spat out the penny and caught it in pinched fingers. With a flick of the copper coin, I snapped open the couplings on the trap's back, just like old times, albeit under greater pressure than when I had been a kid. I slipped the penny under my tongue. Timidly did I crouch and, with closed eyes, reach my fluttering hands in the direction of her gilled cephalothorax. I lifted her from the murky depths with ghostly-white grip and fixed on her stalked ocular. She reached out and touched my mouth with the ripper, not the crusher, and I understood the message. I grabbed her claw and, with one great clip, made quick work of the rope tethering my knotted leg, then cast the lobster and her babies away to the bay. I kicked away the sodden surface of suboceanic earth. The suction of the mud, conserved as energy from the instant I had been thrust up to the calves in the stuff, supplied the explosion that jettisoned me powerfully back to the surface, where I gasped for big gulps of fresh air.

Loony Levis had left Long Wharf, but as a precaution I swam across the channel to the World Trade Center pier. Back on land, I felt rejuvenated. Plumbing the old powers of escape had been exhilarating. Revived, reunited with One Cent, I conjured the adolescent mystic and concentrated on the coin. I didn't care whether it brought me good luck or bad. I needed a sign, and I found it on the back of the penny. "Say no more, Abe, I'm on my way."

Levis had given me something to fight against, something to save; Lincoln showed me where to go next. I checked the watch on my wrist. The old sucker still ticked. Waterproof, it too had survived, but time was running out. I knew the oxygen in Dig City was at that instant winnowing to Everest-thin, my people packing up, resigned to desert all we had worked so hard to build. I had lost an essential hour in the midst of my self-immolating tirade and the run-in with resurrected Levis. That laughing Lazarus, my non-father, had twice tried to sink me when Dig City required rescue from a hostile aggressor. First it had been Miss Spinks, now it was my old nemesis, Apple Jack.

The outage had left stoplights blinking, and badge cats

blew brash whistles while at their intersection pirouettes, but nothing could touch me. I was an invisible ninja slipping through the Beast. Nobody paid attention to me, even with my wild, disheveled aspect, because this was where the dispossessed went to be themselves. I was on the street, in the game. Flared nostrils took lusty snorts of freedom. Long ago, the locals must have felt a little this way—right here, on these weary cobblestones—when the Brits went home having soiled their redcoats and the Yanks knew for certain they were no longer colonists. Shivering, dripping, trailing a remnant of rope, I made sorcerer's tracks through the landscape of past dramas. I sensed rather than saw these places. It was as if I passed more through moments than spaces.

Here I am at the Kendall Square candy factory the day Levis offers up his decoy, Jocy's love child, in backhanded payoff for a barbaric bet with Apple Jack. On the Common, a crowd has gathered near the stump of the old hanging tree. Whom are they watching? Me, twisting myself up in a pretzel, slipping out of miniature manacles, tearing and repairing a sucker's G-note as my conniving colleagues watch the watchers fondle their wallets. Here I am in front of the Federal Reserve, hypnotized by portentous patterns in poured concrete, the moment my fate is sealed, hermetically, as one of trickster. Here I am standing accursed on Metzger's stoop, the blurt of his security door buzzing above the curb where I will be shoved into deceit's back seat, a long black limousine ride that inaugurates my precocious death-longing. Here I am at Quincy Market, where that madman Mano makes me run for my life and, by the chase, gives me the contest of my career.

Standing behind the rank of granite columns at the code-access entrance of the Custom House, I felt for the touch pad, put my fingers on the home row, and typed five characters. For an instant, as the portal started to slide open, I considered tenderly old man Corrente, who had made my name the key to all the toilets all over the Beast and the Northeast. Then in the entrance I saw a hulking shape and heard a voice that, like three others that fateful day, was recognizable but unwelcome: "¿Que pasa, Sasquatch?"

I had narrowly escaped Levis only to fall right into Mano's hands. He palmed my skull like he had done the basketball. The hacker-trafficker had finally caught me, and it was right at the site where we had left off. Had he been laying in wait all these years for me to return to the scene?

"It's a wonder nobody tried to crack the sewage system before," Mano mused, "with a password as parsed as EDDIE."

"You can do whatever you want with me, Mano, but first you've got to give me a few minutes."

Mano gave my head a couple of quarter-turns, right and then left. "Looks like you lost your glasses." He held a smelly foot right under my nose. It was one of those big, grizzly Nikes. "Remember these?"

"I'm sorry about stealing the shoes, okay? I won't run this time."

"Aw, I wasn't mad."

"Yeah, right. The way you've chased me, you're out for blood."

"I was just going to offer you a job, but you were too fast, Eddie."

How was I going to get rid of this sicko? "This is bigger than the two of us. I'm talking about the survival of the underground."

"I know. That's why I'm here, too."

"What do you mean?"

"Apple Jack isn't budging with the juice," Mano said. "Someone has to save Dig City from the stranglehold."

I squinted. Did I have the right man? Everything above-ground seemed upside down. Levis, alleged progenitor, had tried for the second time to snuff me; now here, appearing solicitous, was my prototypical predator. "Why should I trust you?"

Mano leaned close, the corners of his mouth turned down in a dour frown of determination, and gave my cranium a squeeze. "Because my mama's down there."

Awestruck, I squeaked, "I never knew."

"I'm pretty private about my bio. Kind of like you." Mano let go of the ball. "Come on, Eddie: I'll be your eyes."

If there was anybody who had the programming chops to help me throw a wrench in the works it was Mano, the high holy hacker and bishop of cybertropics. He had melted security systems a hell of a lot icier than the water works'. From what I, myopic, could make out, a great tangle of copper piping and diverter valves covered the Custom House walls and ceilings. It had been built to last back in 1838, but it had taken about two hundred years for Pauly Corrente, the godfather of modern plumbing, to put the Doric temple to use as his vault for blackmail by brown water. Mano sat me down at a shrine in the middle of floor: a single monitor atop the black box that contained the mainframe for public works. In a touch that made this outpost just like home, Pauly had put a toilet in front of the term.

Mano flicked on the monitor. The blueprints to the sewers

blossomed on the screen like a fuzzy dream. Everything I had found important up to now had come from Shep, the first fosterer. Suddenly I discovered, at the turning point in my people's lives, that the decoy 'rents, the Correntes, had something to offer the situation. You might have thought it was genetic, that genius that moved me as if involuntarily. Maybe it was Pauly's fresh ghost passing through me. With Mano's help reading the fine print, I sealed off the entrances to the Ted Williams and took control of the sprinkler system. While the tunnel was flooding, Mano ciphered the master password, making it possible for him to maintain complete control of the TW pumps from any term in the city. In a few minutes, the tunnel was filled with water. Clutching One Cent, I chuckled in diabolical satisfaction at the giant exclamation point that popped up on the monitor, along with the ominous inquiry: ARE YOU SURE YOU WANT TO DO THIS?

"What do you think, Eddie? Can the Bees take it?"

"Dig City's tunnels are built on pillars drilled forty feet into bedrock and waterproof to between five and ten feet below the floor. Slurry forty inches thick, reinforced by I-beams twenty-five feet long, goes down to 120 feet. Dig City is like a nuclear submarine. So far, the Bees haven't even fired pigeon shot, but now there's a warhead ready for launch. As long as we alert them to shut the doors, they won't suffer any side effects. There's someone you've got to contact and personally deliver the password to, Mano—fast."

"Terry—I'll tell him." Mano said, marching away.

"You know Terry?"

"I've got news for you, Eddie." One foot out the door, Mano called, "I'm Hermanito."

"Holy shit!"

"Good luck, bro." The portal slammed. When Terry got the message, we would be ready to deal Apple Jack a royal flush.

Our hack was based on the problem that gives the master plumber one of his most lucrative fixes: back-siphonage. Fluid inside a pipe can go either way, and, as long as it's toward lower pressure, flow will continue once the direction is established. This holds true for plumbing of household or citywide proportions. In the Beast's case, effecting the reversal would be as easy as bypassing a few valves. After sepsis had been coaxed to flow backwards, drains would spout dreck like faucets without handles. The Bees would take a deep breath; the brighter Beastonites, meanwhile, would have to hold their bladders and noses. Water—as long as it was gray or shadier—would keep flowing up. The brown water assault could be waged for weeks, but we probably wouldn't need more than a few hours. The Beast would surely blink. Flummoxed, the fat cats would plead for a meeting and, noses pinched, legs crossed, be forced to accept the Dig City Piss Treaty. "ARE YOU SURE YOU WANT TO DO THIS?"

A lips-like icon appeared at the edge of the screen and the term said, in its emotionless stacatto: "Apple Jack would like to chat. Are you presaged to engage?"

Godfather from the machine! I figured: Why not watch the worm squirm? "Sure!"

Apple Jack launched into a rabid rap. His sepulchral voice, threatening to blow out the term's tinny speakers, boomed up to the Custom House dome. "Flooding the tunnel's a clever trick—and with my fresh water, you flat-footed prick. But if you think this will help the Bees survive, you're already oxygen deprived!"

On the monitor, all I could make out was the grinding gilt hole that an hour earlier had breathed fire on me and Metzger in our chimera disguise. Without a doubt, if it had been in the house, that mouth would have prefered to chew me up and spit me out. "Listen to this, Apple Jack: The TW is like an enormous toilet tank, and the pressure drop beneath the Beast is set to suck a monster of an excremental cocktail from the central sewage treatment plant. In seconds, downtown will be inundated with sewage, and you won't be able to reverse the flow until I give Dig City intelligence the say-so."

"I knew this Eddie, about the john, but you don't know what you're sitting on. The second you give the flush command, the bilge will shoot right up your can!" I scrutinized the stats and saw that he was right. The Custom House was locked around me like a safe and the throne on which I sat was the detonator of my own bomb. If I went through with the plan, it would take less than a second for a black sea of terror to be rising above my ears. "There's no way out of this shit bath, and the pressure will rip your ass in half. No matter what the mojo in your feet—in case you didn't notice you're stuck to the seat!"

The suction had grabbed me like a hydra. Apple Jack had me by the actual balls. It was a death trap, a system glitch. I sat at the vortex of my own dunk-swish. In an effort to disarm him, I spouted, "Levis lives!"

"I know what gives. Levis's hep. He knew he was cuckold-kept, and therefore that his wife's first kid couldn't be nothing that he did. Levis cheated, and tried to get away with giving old AJ counterfeit pay. . . ."

On standby, glued to my commode, I was Apple Jack's

captive audience as he retold the story. He was gassing on just to stall, all the while behind the scenes scrambling to see how he might plug my plan, but I had my hand on the handle. The Beast's water main was a virtual vacuum, and I was ready to switch the direction of flow with a single keystroke.

". . . But he didn't know Dig City's spy-man was there to bust his luckless hymen. When Jocy, she gave birth to Mano, Terry went up on the wharf and fished around until he found himself a little baby orphan."

"Then Jocy's not my mother!"

"You're just a shill for Little Brother. Cray made the switch in the baby cage and, just like Levis, my repo agent—"

"Shep?"

"Correct: Shep Veils—neither one knew heads from tails. But like extra ace or ill-suited jack dealt from the bottom of the pack, you came back to haunt the finks with that attack on old Miss Spinks. Cray and Terry hunched something when they saw behemoth feet. Then Jocy knew you bumped the King, making fate complete."

"How'd she get the jist?"

"That faux Rolex on your wrist."

"So when she and I had kids. . . ?"

"In your dreams is where you'd pucker!"

"You mean. . . ?"

"Jocy's not your mother, brother, and you didn't fuck her."

I had been twice trumped. My identity had been snatched, the pocket of my subconscious picked.

"I know who the real folks are. In fact, we're outside in the car."

The sound of rapid pulse overflowed in my ears. An

instant message in full-screen type burst onto the monitor: DC IS SEALED.

"Well, Eddie, you've always known that you're somebody's son. Aren't you dying to see where it is that you come from?" That's when I got a pinch from Lincoln. Trembling, I held the penny an inch from my iris. On the face, I could make out the levity of a president's etched determination. It was there in his furrowed forehead, the rakish angle of his bow tie, in the furtive whorls of his goateed chin and scalloped scalp—almost a Mohawk, now that I looked closely. Abraham Lincoln: proto-punk. "Show your cards, make up your mind: a dead-end surge or long-lost find. Choose your move 'fore I grow old. What'll it be, E? Flush or fold?"

With downcurled mouth, Abe seemed to speak, his profile facing East, back towards besieged Dig City; I read his lips: Free the Bees. I touched index finger to mouth in a brief, baffled vigil; somewhere down there back where my body was supposed to lie: the lobster. Her kiss had split my bottom lip. There was blood on my fingertip. All my children were ready to be released.

"ARE YOU SURE YOU WANT TO DO THIS?"

I flipped One Cent and hit Enter. The pop of a porcelain starter's pistol. The feculent flora of fresh ordure. A great, tumbling, gushing tide of sepsis. I trusted that my new eyes, beady, mounted on pedicels, would show me where to go.

Also from Akashic Books :

Manhattan Loverboy by Arthur Nersesian
203 pages, paperback
ISBN: 1-888451-09-2
Price: $13.95
"Nersesian's newest novel is paranoid fantasy and fantastic comedy in the
service of social realism, using the methods of L. Frank Baum's *Wizard of Oz*
or Kafka's *The Trial* to update the picaresque urban chronicles of Augie
March, with a far darker edge..." —*Downtown Magazine*

Adios Muchachos by Daniel Chavarría
245 pages, paperback
ISBN: 1-888451-16-5
Price: $13.95
"Daniel Chavarría has long been recognized as one of Latin America's finest
writers. Now he again proves why with *Adios Muchachos*, a comic mystery
peopled by a delightfully mad band of miscreants, all of them led by a
woman you will not soon forget—Alicia, the loveliest bicycle whore in all
Havana." —Edgar Award-winning author William Heffernan

Outcast by José Latour
(Nominated for Edgar, Anthony Awards)
217 pages, trade paperback ISBN: 1-888451-07-6
Out of print. First edition copies: $20 (Available only through direct
mail order.)
"José Latour is a master of Cuban Noir, a combination of '50s unsentimental-
ity and the harsh realities of life in a Socialist paradise. Better, he brings his
tough survivor to the States to give us a picture of ourselves through Cuban
eyes. Welcome to America, Sr. Latour."
—Martin Cruz Smith, author of *Havana Bay*

The Big Mango by Norman Kelley
270 pages, trade paperback
ISBN: 1-888451-10-8
Price: $14.95
She's Back! Nina Halligan, Private Investigator.
"Want a scathing social and political satire? Look no further than Kelley's
second effort featuring 'bad girl' African-American PI and part-time intellec-
tual Nina Halligan—it's X-rated, but a romp of a read . . . Nina's acid takes on
recognizable public figures and institutions both amuse and offend . . . Kelley
spares no one, blacks and whites alike, and this provocative novel is sure to
attract attention . . ." —*Publisher's Weekly*

Kamikaze Lust by Lauren Sanders
287 pages, trade paperback
ISBN: 1-888451-08-4
Price: $14.95
"Like an official conducting an all-out strip search, first-time novelist Lauren Sanders plucks and probes her characters' minds and bodies to reveal their hidden lusts, and when all is said and done, nary a body cavity is spared." —*Time Out New York*

Heart of the Old Country by Tim McLoughlin
216 pages, trade paperback
ISBN: 1-888451-15-7
Price: $14.95
"*Heart of the Old Country* is a wise and tender first novel, though its youthful narrator would surely not like to hear that said. His boisterous, irreverent, often hilarious tough-guy pose is his armor, for he comes from the heart of old Brooklyn, where compassion and emotion are considered fatal weaknesses. Yet underneath it all, he shows a love for humanity so deep it might equal Dostoevksy's. Tim McLoughlin is a master storyteller in the tradition of such great New York City writers as Hubert Selby Jr. and Richard Price. I can't wait for his second book!"
 —Kaylie Jones, author of *A Soldier's Daughter Never Cries*

These books are available at local bookstores. They can also be purchased with a credit card online through www.akashicbooks.com. To order by mail, or to order out-of-print titles, send a check or money order to:

Akashic Books
P.O. Box 1456
New York, NY 10009
www.akashicbooks.com
Akashic7@aol.com
(Prices include shipping. Outside the U.S., add $3 to each book ordered.)

Robert Arellano was born in Summit, New Jersey to Alicia Maria Belt y de Cardenas and Manuel Enrique Maria Ramirez de Arellano. *Fast Eddie, King of the Bees* is his first print novel. As the alias Bobby Rabyd, he created the Internet's first interactive novel, *Sunshine '69*, published by Sonicnet in 1996. Experience the digital narrative at sunshine69.com. Arellano lives in Cranston, Rhode Island and teaches hypertext fiction and Cuban studies at Brown University. When touring and recording with Bonny Prince Billy, Arellano uses only Gibson guitars.

Marek Bennett grew up in Henniker, New Hampshire and studied at Brown University in Providence, Rhode Island. His works include the serial sci-fi comic *Quasar Blasters* and an illustrated history, *The Squirrel Wars*.